JULIETTE'S VAN GOGH

A Seekers After Lost Treasure Adventure

C.L.DECKER

with C.A.SCRIBNER

Shadow Rock

This book is a work of fiction. Although places mentioned and descriptions are real, characters, names, and incidents are fiction. Resemblance to any events or persons, living or dead, is purely coincidental, except for the artists mentioned and their works. See the Facts and Fiction section at the end of this book.

Juliette's Van Gogh. Copyright © 2019 by C.L.Decker

Cover illustration and design by Kathleen Kinkopf, kinkopfdesign.com/kinkopfstudios.com

Portrait art by Enrico Embroli, enricoembrolistudios.com

Shadow Rock Publishing logo by Edward Fong, e-modernegallerie.com

ISBN 978-0-578-61314-7

Library of Congress Cataloging-in-Publication Data is available upon request.

Published by Shadow Rock Publishing, LLC

165 Shadow Rock Drive, Sedona, AZ 86336.

Printed in the United States of America.

Dedicated to our loving

international family

CONTENTS

As if a blind man is searching

in a dark room

for a black cat

that isn't there.

– Unknown

PROLOGUE

PARIS

An unmarked white panel van travels slowly on the curving road through the countryside, heading toward Paris. Vast fields of grazing cattle and flourishing crops once lined the roadway, but all that remain are scattered stone farmhouses, intermixed with small industrial parks of corrugated-metal warehouses. Occasionally the van passes large brick buildings built during the war; some are derelict, but others are still used as storage spaces.

Earsplitting punk rock music spills out from the open windows of the van. Over the music, the lone passenger, an armed guard named Joseph, shouts, "Pull off! I need a smoke."

"We're not supposed to stop for anything!" bitches Gus, the driver, without letting up on the gas. He quickly grumbles, "What the hell, I need to stretch my legs before we hit the Paris traffic ... and I need a drag."

A short distance down the narrow road, Gus pulls off on a patch of gravel along the shoulder and stops. They both climb out of the van and promptly light up. "I've been thinking ..."

"Not healthy, Gus," Joseph snarls through a puff of smoke.

"What's with the small crated piece we picked up at that old olive farm outside Arles? Why is it going to Amsterdam?" Gus mumbles without disturbing the Gauloises dangling from his lips. "I know the art that the institute is shipping to the Pompidou has got to be worth something ... but art from a farmhouse?"

"When did you start wondering about what we're carrying? I have no idea and I don't really care." Joseph drops his cigarette and crushes it into the gravel with the heel of his shoe. "I just have to get it there safely. So let's get outta here, allez, allez," he says, gesturing toward the van.

A few miles down the road, Gus notices a tow truck pulling up fast from the rear. It seems to have come from nowhere and is picking up speed. "If this guy doesn't slow down, he's going to ram right into us!" Gus yells, watching in the rearview mirror with trepidation. Before he finishes his words, the truck has pulled around their van, cut right in front of them, and slammed on the brakes.

Gus screams, "What the hell?" as he brakes hard, but not in time to avoid a collision.

The hard jerk of their seat belts leaves them momentarily stunned. Gus is the first to recover and says with disgust, "Shit! We're screwed."

Two figures in gas masks jump out of the tow truck, carrying what look like fire extinguishers. One comes to each side of the van and through the open windows sprays the inside of the van before either Joseph or Gus can do anything. Gus would later report that all he remembered was a slight sickly-sweet smell before he blacked out.

The two assailants drag Joseph and Gus out of the van, then pull off their gas masks. They bind Gus and Joseph with zip ties, then gag and blindfold them. "We need to throw them in the back of the van fast, before someone comes along and sees us," barks one of the assailants. They stack them between the

2

wrapped and crated art in the back of the van. One closes up the van while the other hooks up the tow bar to its frame. They jump back into the truck and tear down the road with the van in tow.

About thirty minutes closer to Paris, they turn off the paved road onto a dusty lane. Broken chunks of pavement lead up a slight grade to an abandoned brick warehouse in the midst of an unkempt field. The windows are all broken out. The large doors that once were at each end are long since gone. The wooden roof is partially collapsed, and the interior scavenged of all usable materials. "There's our ride," the shorter of the assailants says, pointing to a black SUV parked just outside the warehouse. They pass by the SUV and pull straight into the warehouse. The driver of the SUV gets out and opens the rear hatch, then joins the other two in the warehouse.

"How'd it go?" he asks.

"So far, so good" was the quick answer.

They open up the back of the van and remove the bodies of the two unconscious men, dropping them away from the van on the concrete floor. They remove the crate marked for Amsterdam and carry it to the black SUV, putting it carefully inside. As the two assailants turn to re-enter the warehouse, they see that the blindfold on one of the men they had gassed has partially slipped off and he's hobbling toward a side exit. "Damn, where's he going?" At the sound of the assailant's voice, the man instinctively hesitates and looks right into the faces of both assailants. "Merde, he's seen us!"

The other assailant runs and grabs one of the gas canisters from the back of the open van and in a few steps reaches the hobbled man. He smashes the canister into his skull. The man crumbles to the floor. A small puddle of blood oozes from the wound. Both assailants kneel down next to the body. "Is he dead?" one asks the other.

3

"Well, his skull is bashed in." He feels for a pulse. "Yeah … he's not going to identify anybody."

"Throw him into the SUV. We'll get rid of him later." The two assailants pick up the body and toss it into the back of the SUV alongside the Amsterdam crate.

"Get the gasoline can out of the truck … let's get this job done and get out of here."

As the other assailant grabs the can from the cab of the truck and starts splashing it over the tow truck and the van, the man on the ground slowly stirs, still tied, gagged, and blindfolded. He hears splashing and smells gasoline fumes. He hears a loud swoosh and instantly feels heat from the fire as the van and tow truck are engulfed in flames. In terror, he rolls as far as he can from the heat.

As the two assailants climb into the SUV, one screams to the driver, "Vite, vite."

Before he pulls away, the driver asks, "Did you throw the GPS tracker monitor and gas masks in the truck so they'd be destroyed?"

"Yes, yes. You think I'm stupid? Get moving!"

....

It seems forever to the man on the ground before he hears the sound of sirens in the distance. He prays that they are on their way to find him. He is sweating from the intense heat of the fire. He smells burning rubber and hears frequent explosive pops in the fire. The sounds, smells, and intense heat are terrifying. The ties on his wrists and ankles are cutting into his skin like blades. He wonders if this is the end as he mercifully drifts back into unconsciousness.

....

His fuzzy mind seems to hear voices, but he isn't sure if he's just dreaming. He feels someone remove the ties and then at last his blindfold. He opens his eyes and blinks a few times and then looks around. Firefighters are everywhere, and the van and truck are still smoldering. He looks at the scene more intently, then starts shouting, "Joseph! Joseph!" The firefighter kneeling next to him quietly says, "I'm sorry, but there's no one else here."

Joseph was gone.

JULIETTE'S VAN GOGH

Chapter 1: THE OLIVE FARM

ARLES – One week earlier

The Martines' olive farm had been in the family for over 250 years. The old, gnarled olive trees marked the years as accurately as a time capsule. Nestled into the hillsides outside Arles, the rolling acres of land encircled a small stone farmhouse. Barn and out-buildings, took on a golden hew in the early-morning light, reminiscent of a scene out of a Monet painting, complete with shadows cast by the rising sun. The leaves of the olive trees fluttered in the breeze, revealing their paler green underside. In a certain light, they appeared to be silver in color.

The Martine family, with the help of neighbors and itinerant workers, still harvested their olives. They sold most to local exporters but pressed some into olive oil at the communal facility in town, selling a portion and keeping the rest for their own use. Today was going to be an unusual day for them. Instead of the day-to-day routine of operating the farm, they would welcome a university student from the Sorbonne, in Paris. He was a stranger to the family who had said in a phone call that he wanted to talk to them about an ancestor of theirs, Juliette Martine. They had no idea what to expect, but at least it would be a change of pace.

....

Dean Nixon squeezed into his twentyfive-year-old Citroën 2CV—or deux chevaux (two horses), as the car was often called—and was grateful that it started. The old, rusted car was unreliable, but it was all he could afford. With a master's degree in psychology, he was working on his PhD in fine art at the Sorbonne. His still-in-progress dissertation was titled, "The Psychological Relationships of an Artist to Friends, Patrons, and Models," using Van Gogh as an example. With a PhD, he'd be ready for a real job—and the dream of eventually opening his own gallery in his home town, New York. Studying at the university had used up his meager inheritance from his grandparents a couple of years before. He was down to his last euros.

He had recently found, in Van Gogh's letters to his brother Theo, references to a favorite model in Arles named Juliette Martine. This was the sort of relationship that was essential to his dissertation, and he longed for more information on Juliette. Taking advantage of the voluminous ancestral material now available on the internet, Dean had been able to find a Martine family related to Juliette still living near Arles. Follow-up digging produced a rural address for Gaston and Adrienne Martine. After a phone call to the Arles mairie, or town hall, and a friendly conversation with Beatrice, a helpful clerk, he had a phone number. Two days later, he was on his way to his appointment to interview the Martine family.

He had arrived from Paris late the previous night after the long drive to Arles and had checked into a local hostel, trying to stretch his dwindling euros. This morning, as he approached the farm in his deux chevaux, he was impressed with the solid blanket of olive groves surrounding the family home. Studying in Paris with limited means had meant that he hadn't had the opportunity to explore the French countryside. A day trip to Versailles hardly counted.

8

As he pulled up in front of the farmhouse, laced with dense red roses and lush green vines that clung greedily to the old stone walls, the front door opened and out stepped a middle-aged man. He was dressed in patched and faded work clothes and heavy boots. An old leather belt with extra holes punched in it held his pants around his thinning waist. His skin was dark and wrinkled from years working under the sun, and he looked older than his sixty-odd years. He greeted Dean with a strong grip and introduced himself, "Hello, you must be Mr. Nixon. I'm Gaston Martine. Welcome to our home."

"It's so kind of you to give me this opportunity to meet with you and your family. Please call me Dean."

Gaston responded with a wide smile and ushered Dean over the well-worn tread of the threshold and into his humble home. He took Dean directly to the kitchen, the heart of their home, and introduced him to his wife, Adrienne. She wore a flowered print apron trimmed in bright blue braiding over her colorless cotton dress. Her house slippers shuffled softly on the polished stone tiles that covered the kitchen floor. They had been worn smooth by centuries of tired feet that had carried the women of the family as they fed both the family and the field workers. Adrienne too greeted Dean warmly. "I've just taken some brioche from the oven. Can I offer you a slice, with some coffee?" she asked as she cut the sweet-smelling bread into thick, soft slices.

"That would be wonderful," he responded as he pulled up a chair at the richly oiled wooden kitchen table.

As the three sipped their steaming hot coffee and slathered the brioche with fresh butter and globs of homemade fruit preserves, Dean told them about his dissertation. He explained the story that he wanted to tell through his work. He was hoping to shed light on the unique emotional relationships between great

9

artists and their patrons, friends, and very importantly, their models. Surprisingly to Dean, they both listened with rapt attention and even asked questions. And he had yet to even mention Juliette.

Gaston helped himself to another coffee. "You said on the phone that you were especially interested in Van Gogh? We're all very proud of him in Arles, you know, but it didn't seem like his life was very happy here."

"Well, I'm using him as my main artist, to look at the relationships throughout his life. That is how I found the name Juliette Martine. From what I've been able to find so far, it seems that she was a favorite model of Van Gogh's while he worked here in Arles. I'm very anxious to learn anything I can about her life and work with him. That's how I came to search for any family history. I was so excited to learn on the internet that you existed ... that the Martine family still existed. To find you still here on the family farm is like a dream come true for me." He found himself feeling a true warmth for these two people, who no longer felt like strangers.

"Oh, I hope we don't disappoint you, Dean." Gaston leaned forward toward Dean as if to reassure him. "We don't know much about this Juliette except old family gossip—that she was a model for an artist. No one ever said his name, that we know of. We all just thought it was an old wives' tale that people like to pass on. Guess we always thought it was a nice story we just liked to dream about, to make our ordinary lives feel a little special."

Dean pulled out the ancestral chart he had drawn up from his online research and unfolded it on the kitchen table. "You can see her name right here," he said, moving his finger through the names on the chart. He stopped when he got to Gaston's name. "And here you are, Gaston. She really existed, just as you exist."

10

Gaston and Adrienne leaned in close. Their eyes grew wide as they studied the diagram and read the names as decades played out the family history. They paused when they got to Gaston's name and looked at each other with tear-filled eyes. Here were Gaston's roots, and they were right on this piece of paper—not just in stories and fading memories, nearly lost to time.

Gaston reached across the table and lay his weathered hand on Dean's arm. "Thank you for this gift, Dean, it's priceless. We want to help you in any way we can."

Visibly moved by Gaston's response, Dean laid his hopes out on the table. "Well, in his letters to his brother Theo, Vincent described Juliette as his favorite model and companion. I was hoping that there might be some documents, old bibles, or family stories that might help me."

"For a start, let me bring in Gaston's mother, Agnes." Adrienne pushed back her chair and got up from her place at the table. "If anyone has any idea, it would be her. I'll just go get her." A few minutes later, she returned to the kitchen with an elderly woman walking slowly with a cane for support. "This is Agnes," she told Dean, introducing her as she helped her settle into the chair right next to him. "She just turned ninety-three and remembers a lot about the family from the old days."

"Agnes, this is Dean Nixon. He wants to know about the Juliette you've talked about and the artist she posed for," Adrienne said, speaking a little more loudly to be sure Agnes heard clearly.

Agnes softly took Dean's hand and squeezed it. "I'm pleased to meet you, Dean."

Dean was surprised at how firmly she had taken his hand for such a frail-looking woman. "Thank you for joining us," he said, firmly squeezing her hand in kind. "I understand that you remember a lot about the family history."

"I'm not so sure about that anymore. My memory isn't what it once was, but I'd like to help you if I can. What do you want to know?"

"Do you remember hearing any details about Juliette and the artist she posed for? Maybe some stories, or do you know of any letters that may have any information about Juliette?"

"I remember hearing some stories, but I don't remember any details. I think my sister-in-law, Sadie, still has some old papers that have been handed down." Looking hopefully into Dean's eyes, she said, "Maybe there will be something there that could help you?"

"Fantastic!" Dean wanted to jump out of his chair, he was so excited. "Anything would be a great help. How can I get to see them?"

"Sadie lives just up the road." Agnes smiled at his youthful energy. "If she still has them, they would probably be in her attic. We'll call her right now!"

Sadie welcomed their call and invited Gaston to bring Dean straight over to visit. Any company at her age was welcome, especially here in the countryside.

Dean said his goodbyes to Adrienne and Agnes, and as he left the farmhouse with Gaston, he promised them that he'd share anything he learned about the family.

....

Sadie's cottage turned out to be on the other side of the olive groves. She had never married and had chosen to live in a family cottage that had been occupied by several generations of the Martine family before her. Perhaps because she never had children of her own, she had become the family historian and had collected and protected all sorts of family records.

"Welcome, Dean, it's a pleasure to meet you. I hope that I can help you." Sadie welcomed Dean into her home without a moment of hesitation. She moved about without any assistance and appeared more fit than Agnes, even though she was the older of the two.

"Sadie, would you show Dean your attic so he can see what you have stored?" Gaston spoke quickly now, anxious to learn what more could be discovered about his family.

"Of course. Please follow me, will you?"

Dean and Gaston followed Sadie up a narrow set of stairs to a door that led to a small, dusty room under the eaves with only one window. A single light bulb hung from a cord over their heads.

"Well, here it is. You can see I don't spend much time here. If there's anything to be found about Juliette, it would be up here."

"This is amazing," said Dean as he scanned the dimly lit room. It was stuffed with old furniture, crates, cardboard boxes, newspapers, and a few trunks. "It's going to take me some time to work my way through all this. Will you allow me that opportunity?"

"Please be my guest. In fact, I have an extra bedroom if you'd like to make yourself at home for a few days."

"That's very generous of you, but I have a room in Arles. If it's all right with you, I'll just commute from there. Is it okay if I begin right now?"

"Dig in," she said, gesturing to the piles of boxes and trunks. "Let me know if you need anything. And I insist you join me later for lunch." Not pausing for a response, she turned to leave the room and told Gaston to come get a stool to bring upstairs for Dean to use. Dean wasted no time and knelt down to open the first box, blowing thick dust off the top before he opened it.

After sorting for a few hours through piles of old parchment, birth certificates, death notices, and deeds,

Dean joined Sadie in the kitchen for a lunch of white bean soup with fresh tomatoes, onions, and herbs—all from the same garden, no doubt—and a small glass of the family's white wine, made from local grapes. He enjoyed her company, as she was an unusually interesting lady, but he was so anxious to get back to the hunt that he quickly sopped up the last of the rich broth in his bowl with a thick slice of Sadie's crusty French bread, warm from her oven. Sadie never missed a note. "Go get back to it, Dean. You're on a mission, so don't waste your time down here with me. Whatever you find will be wonderful for us too ... if there is indeed anything to be found."

Dean searched for hours, taking his time so he was certain not to miss any important piece of paper. It was starting to get dark outside, and it became harder to make out the words on a page with the faint evening light coming through the single window. It was growing dimmer by the minute, with only the single bulb to offer him light now. Dean was exhausted. He was almost at the bottom of an old crate when he found a small bound book. Its cover was made of a dark canvas-like fabric, with leather trim. There had been something written on the cover, but it had faded with use and time, so he couldn't read it. He carefully opened it and began to turn the pages. It appeared to be poetry, free verse in style. The French gave him no challenge as he skimmed the pages. As he turned the next page, he found writing on the back side of the page he had just turned. It was upside down, but he could see clearly it was in another person's hand. He turned a couple more pages and found the same. He paused, then excitedly turned the book over and began to look at it from the back cover, reading the back side of each page.

He could hardly breathe. "Could it be?" he said to himself. It looked to be in a woman's hand, at least

14

to his untrained eye. He turned another page and there it was … Juliette Martine's diary, telling her story.

Juliette's Diary

April 15, 1888

It's cold, damp, and musty-smelling in my little room. One small, grimy window looks out over the alley below. The room is just big enough for my sagging bed, a tired chair worn through in some places to the stuffing, and a rickety wooden washstand I found on the street. My one small comfort is a tatty old quilt my grand-mère made me when I was a little girl living on our olive farm near Arles. When I wrap myself in it, as I am now, I imagine that I can smell her lavender scent and hear the family warming themselves by the fire in the old farmhouse kitchen. Those were good days in my life … hard but good. The once bright colors of the quilt—the deep blue of the bluebells, the bright red of the poppies, the warm yellow at the hearts of the daisies in our fields between the rows of green-leafed olive trees—are faded now, but it warms me well as I write.

My little piece of luck, a young man who said he was a poet left one of his writing books and ink in my room, so I gain from his forgetfulness. I like to write in my new book. It gives me a place to put down my words that no one else would care to hear and that I'd choose not to share. Words let me see myself, see my life now and try to figure out how I feel about it all. Although I've never seen one, I think that this is what they call a diary.

I finally have a job that doesn't require me to lie on my back and give pleasure to grunting, sweaty, bad-smelling men. A fortnight ago I met a young man in the tavern. "Vincent van Gogh is my name," he said to me as we began talking. At first, I thought him to be just another man that I would service and earn some coin from. But after a time, he told me he was an artist who had trouble selling his paintings and thereby did not have much money to pay for my usual services. He did, however, ask me to pose for him while he paints pictures of me on his canvas (a new word to me), in return for a smaller sum.

He is not what I'd call handsome, but he's not ugly either. He has a full head of unruly red hair and a trimmed red beard, and sometimes in the light his eyes are the beautiful green color on the top side of our olive leaves. He seems to be a gentle sort. He told me he once was a minister like his father. This new work with Vincent doesn't pay much, but something, and everything helps. Maybe I can see less of the other men.

I found his rented room over a restaurant small but much larger than mine. Though bright and colorful, it feels a bit sad. His bed is just big enough for the two of us, when we choose to rest together. There is a small painted table with two chairs, his easel, and a corner stand covered with his paint tins. I don't mind him looking at my naked body while he paints. It's so different then when I am in bed with the other men.

April 16, 1888

I modeled for Vincent today, that's what he told me it's called when you hold a position for hours while an artist like him paints on a canvas what he sees. That word 'canvas,' it just means a piece of linen stretched over some pieces of wood with their edges cut and glued together. At times, like today, he seems a little moody and fickle, but not in a scary way. I mean he's quieter and he gets angry when I need to stretch my body while I'm posing. Days like today he doesn't touch me. He makes me feel like I'm no more than a chair in the room.

Even though he knows what I do for a living, he is really very kind to me, even gentle and caring. During breaks he gently covers my naked body with a light blanket, offers me a small glass of wine or, when it's very cold, a hot black coffee.

When we finished today, he told me he didn't need me for the next week or so. I am disappointed because I enjoy him.

May 24, 1888

    Still posing for Vincent—that's what I call him since that is the way he signs his paintings. We have become closer, and now when we share his bed to rest we touch each other, we have each other. I enjoy Vincent with my hands, my mouth. I give him my body. No, I share my body with Vincent in a way I have never done with any other man. So many new feelings. I think it feels different to Vincent too. He pays me some extra. I would do it for no coin if I didn't need the money so very much to live. He asks me to stop seeing my other men. I tell him I can't, I must do it for the money. He says that he understands but doesn't like it. Sometimes I think that I see a bigger anger inside Vincent. It's like hot, scary feelings inside this man are boiling like the fire in the small stove that heats his room. If he opened his skin, would those feelings shoot out like the flames from the fire when he opens the door to the stove?

    Lately, on pretty days he's been painting outdoors in the orchards and meadows. I sit with him while he paints, and we share a bottle of wine. Some of these paintings are a little strange. To me, the colors are all wrong. Sometimes he likes to mix red and orange; grays and blacks turn blue and green. I don't like it, but he explains that that's how he sees the world. I wonder sometimes if maybe he could be a little mad in his head. My father had a younger brother that always stayed on the farm. He never talked when the family was together, and sometimes he would get wild mad for no reason and scare me. My father said that he was a little mad in his head, but that he was safe and happy enough with us on the farm. I wonder does Vincent have a safe place like the farm?

He tells me he still hasn't sold any paintings. I can see that it makes him very sad. I can understand why. Without the money that his brother Theo sends, he could not survive. I could not survive.

May 29, 1888

Nothing seems to change, except Vincent still can't sell his art and he becomes more and more depressed—another new word he has taught me. It means a very bad sadness. He says he can't get the paintings right. Maybe I should tell him the reason why—the colors are all wrong, his figures and fields look almost ugly—but I keep silent. He talked to me again about his failures during his days as a minister. People fell asleep during his sermons, he told me. His brother Theo was the one who finally told him to follow his passion for art, and he would support him when he needed help.

Late yesterday, he learned that he had at last sold one painting, but for just enough to cover the price of his canvas and paints. He's using me more for sharing my body in his bed now and less for modeling. I don't mind. But he does make me feel guilty, as the little money he pays me comes from the meager amount sent by Theo.

August 15, 1888

He no longer has the funds to pay me. He apologizes and says he'll make it up when his paintings begin to sell. I don't think this will ever come to be. I don't stop coming to him. I'm not sure if it's because I love him or I like to think that he needs me. Now more than ever, he hates my need to have other men, but he has no way to help me, so I must not stop. I think his depression is getting worse.

September 20, 1888

Vincent has finally moved into the little yellow house he has been longing to live in for some time. Now he waits for his artist friend Paul Gauguin to come from Paris to share it with him. He tells me that when Paul arrives, all will be better, and his work will improve. I think he misses this friend very much. Maybe his coming will help Vincent.

I like the new space in the yellow house. It feels like a happier place, at least to me.

The rooms inside have been painted the pretty colors of the rainbow, and there is a small meadow of wildflowers that spread all around the house. The air here is so fresh-smelling, like the scent of the clean, dry sheets when I'd pull them off the line at the farmhouse. Sometimes when Vincent paints outside here, I love to lie in the grasses and feel the heat of the bright, warm sun melt into my skin. I have never known a feeling like this before, this utter calm. I am grateful to Vincent.

Lying there in the warm sun helps me to forget about my damp, musty little room. It lets me feel as if I am more. I don't have words to say what that more is, but I know it is good. Maybe I am more.

October 23, 1888

An important day for Vincent. His friend Paul Gauguin has finally arrived. He will be living and working with Vincent for a while. A long while, I hope, for Vincent.

December 18, 1888

Vincent says that he thought his and Paul's "ideals"—I'm not sure what he means—were so in tune, it would be wonderful to work together. But they began arguing about their different ideals about art from the beginning, and sometimes they have had fights. They have even hurt each other—bruises, small tears in their skin. I have seen men do worse, but I feel sad for them both.

But today began as a good day. A rare summer day in winter. Wrapped in blankets, we shared a lunch together in the meadow, where the wildflowers have now been replaced with winter grasses. Sadly, before we had finished the last of our cheese and wine, Paul told Vincent he'd decided that in order to paint his idea of the "purity" he found in simple people and nature, he needed to work in an "isolated" place. He talked of moving to an island in the South Pacific where he could be true to his spirit. I don't know what some of these words mean, but I do know that Paul feels very strongly about this. I can tell he means to do this at any cost.

Vincent got very angry with Paul when he heard this news and screamed at him that he was

betraying him. Betray, it is a word
full of pain and hurt.

As I cleaned the table in the
meadow after Vincent had gone
inside, Paul told me Vincent is
acting like a madman. He is afraid
for him.

If anyone would know this,
Paul would know. I am afraid. I
am afraid for Vincent. I am afraid
for myself, Juliette. Yes, I am afraid
for Juliette Martine … ME! Vincent is
the first man to show me kindness,
maybe even love, and I think I am
losing him.

December 24, 1888

A terrible day. I arrived at the
house to find Paul packing to leave
for Paris. His hands shook as he
stuffed his paints and clothes into
his bags. I asked him where Vincent
was. He told me Vincent had cut off
part of his ear in a fit of rage after
an argument with him the evening
before and was now in the hospital.

It is happening. I don't know
just what it is, but I know in my
heart that it is very bad.

January 9, 1889

No longer posing for Vincent, I have sadly had to find new customers in order to survive. But today I took some time to visit Vincent at the yellow house. He has finally come home from the hospital. I found him in his studio with his head bandaged. He told me himself that in a fit of rage and depression—that's how he said it to me—he tried to cut off his ear. I had never seen Vincent like this, he was like a cold stone in my arms. My heart hurt for him today. It was as if he had put a knife in my heart and twisted it. I can do nothing for Vincent. I think in his mind he has gone away from me, maybe from everyone. I am lost. I am helpless with Vincent, with myself.

May 18, 1889

A note from Vincent found its way to me today. He told me he had admitted himself to an asylum near Saint-Rémy. It's a special hospital for people who are mad in their heads like Vincent, like my uncle. He tells me in his words that he became afraid of what he might do after trying to cut off his ear. He asks me to visit him. I want to, but I have no money. I will try.

June 20, 1889

I visited Vincent at the asylum yesterday. A sad place in the middle of a beautiful countryside. He told me he feels a little better, but I don't know. He still seemed very depressed. Yet he still paints. Still making his mad images and colors. He showed me a painting he said was a view from his window at night. He called it "Starry Night." The surface of the painting looked rough and crude. He had painted bright rings of light around the stars. I didn't like the painting, but what could I do but say it was beautiful. He smiled at me when I said those words. His smile made my heart hurt. How can I say it … my heart felt as if he had touched it with the flame of a candle. Why can't Vincent see the goodness, the beauty I see in him? How I wish I could know that he sometimes remembers the joy we shared lying in the meadows of Arles, drinking wine and laughing together like the children we once were and would never be again.

When I left Vincent today, my shoulders carried the heavy weight of grief. I had a strong feeling that this would be the last time we would ever be together. I began to cry as we held each other for a tender moment. Vincent has taught me ... he taught me so very much. I turned away and left him standing alone. I didn't want him to see my tears, my pain.

Would he have seen my pain? Or is his pain so full, he cannot see another's pain?

July 23, 1889

To my surprise, a package arrived from Vincent today. I never get packages. I felt like I did as a small child on Noël when I woke in the morning hoping there would be a small gift for me. I slowly unwrapped the cord and brown paper and found a painting and a note, which I laid aside. The sky in the painting is blue and black, but the dark clouds are all the same. The olive trees in the grove don't look normal and are funny colors.

As he always does, Vincent has painted the name on the back. It says "Stormy Day in the Olive Grove" and his name, Vincent van Gogh.

After a while, I open his note. He writes that the painting is a gift to me and is a sister piece to the "Starry Night" painting he showed me when I visited him. He says it is a very stormy sky in an olive grove that might remind me of the one I knew as a child.

I touch the painting tenderly, as I would touch Vincent's skin. Oh, how I want to love this gift, but the colors seem so wrong. The whole painting is scary, and I hate it, but I can't tell him that. It makes me feel Vincent's pain.

Mon Dieu! My breath leaves me. Is that what Vincent is trying to say to me with this painting? I run my fingers across the dark sky. Is he trying to show me, to have me feel his pain, his sorrow? All this time, and I never knew. Can I ask him this? I will hang it here in my small room and think on this. Yes, I must think on this.

His note also says that "Stormy Day" is a gift for all my companionship and modeling, for

which he could not pay. He signs it,
"Fondly, your Vincent."

I think that I will treasure
this note as much as the painting ...
forever.

July 29, 1889

My Vincent died today. They
told me his last moments were in his
brother Theo's arms. I think he
would have liked that. I know now
that this strange man meant
everything to me. I hurt for the loss
of him. But now when I fall asleep
at night, under my quilt, I will
know he suffers no more. There is no
more pain for my Vincent. My tears
are leaving wrinkly spots on the
pages in my book. The ink is
running from my words, melting
into the paper as my heart now
melts into my soul.

I wonder if anyone will ever
see or understand his art. He
seemed to know what he wanted to
say in his paintings but was unable
to get others to see it through his
eyes.

I want to believe that in the
end, in "Stormy Day," I finally saw

it. Maybe in that moment, Vincent,
I finally saw you.

The ink was faded, and sometimes Dean had to guess at words and parts of pages were hard to make out, but her heart was on the page. It was unbelievable. This moment was unbelievable. He was holding it in his hands. She did exist. She had shared her life on these pages. Now he would know it. The family would know it. He was anxious to study it in better light, but first he had to share it with her family.

That night, Dean joined the family around Sadie's old wooden kitchen table and shared the diary. They were all overcome with emotion. Each one held it tenderly in their hands, turning the pages with great care, as Dean had cautioned them, as they read bits and pieces. It was as if they each held a newborn … utterly entranced. After a time, Dean spoke quietly, not wanting to break the mood but needing to make a plan. "I need to spend time with the diary and study the pages I couldn't see well enough to translate. If it's okay with you, Sadie, I'd like to spend tomorrow right here in your well-lit kitchen, doing just that, before I continue to search the attic. I'm staying in a hostel and don't feel that's a safe enough place for such a valuable document."

"Please do what you need to, Dean. We trust you and thank you for this miracle," Sadie said, and they all nodded yes enthusiastically. "We all want to help you in any way we can."

....

The next day Dean spent hunched over the diary in the warm kitchen, not hearing or seeing anyone or anything around him. Gaston and Adrienne came by to see how it was going, and Sadie insisted he take a quick lunch. By the end of the day, he had been able to translate the entire diary … that is, what was legible.

He rewrapped it in a handwoven piece of linen Sadie had found for him the night before, and returned it to a small stone niche that she had shown him in the wall of her sitting room. They had all decided that that was a safe, dry place for the time being. When Dean fell into his bed at the hostel that night, he prayed that he had made the right decision not to mention the painting that evening as he'd left Sadie's house.

....

The next morning, as soon as the sun rose, he was back in the attic. There still was a corner of the attic he had not touched. He started moving the boxes and crates away from the wall, finding old boots, pieces of furniture, and clothing. He finally came to a box that was larger than the other boxes. It had been filled with wadded-up paper as padding. He started pulling the paper out of the box and peered in. There were several picture frames of different sizes. He moved the box so he could get the best light possible in the dim attic. He looked at each picture carefully as he lifted them out of the box, one by one.

Some were old family photos. Some had hand-lettered lists of some sort. Then he saw the words painted on the back of a canvas, "Stormy Day in the Olive Grove," and below it the unmistakable name, Vincent van Gogh. His whole body went numb. He couldn't move. He could barely breathe.

He felt the tears before he realized what they were. "When was the last time I cried?" he asked himself. He bowed his head and breathed carefully as he slowly turned the frame over in his hands, instinctively closing his eyes as he did so. "Can I dare to hope?"

The painting glowed even in this dim light. It was the most beautiful thing Dean had ever seen. He moved it to the attic's only window, where he could see the heavy brush strokes, the stylistic trees and sky, the discordant colors. Breathless, he whispered out loud, "Oh my God! It's Juliette's Van Gogh."

He sat down on the floor, spellbound, and stared at the painting. He finally roused himself and stood, grasping the painting in both hands. It was time to share it with the family.

He carefully carried it down the narrow stairway into the kitchen, where the family was gathered for mid-morning coffee, as if they were waiting for him. He turned the painting around to face them. They froze in place, not sure what to do. Or what to say.

"According to Juliette's diary, shortly before he died, Van Gogh gave her one of his paintings as a gift of thanks. I decided not to tell you before I left last night. I didn't want to give you false hope until I had a chance to look for it today. I feel honored, more than honored, that I was able to find this lost Van Gogh painting. It's called Stormy Day in the Olive Grove, just as she wrote in her diary. And it appears to be in good condition, even after all these years. Let's clear the table and I'll place it there so everyone can get a good look at this masterpiece."

They rapidly cleared the table, allowing him to place the painting in the center, then crowded tightly around to better see it.

"I believe in my heart that it is real," Dean told them. "I believe that it is indeed a Van Gogh! His gift to your Juliette."

Not sure just what to say or ask, overwhelmed and confused, Gaston finally uttered the words everyone but Dean was thinking: "What does this mean?"

"It means you as a family own a very valuable painting, maybe many millions of euros! It's undiscovered and beautiful and seems to be in good physical condition. It would be new to the market, so I think it should bring a spectacular price at auction. But all of this assumes that it can be officially authenticated as having been painted by Van Gogh."

The Martines looked at one another, both numb and a little lost. After a pause, Gaston turned to Dean and asked, "What should we do now?"

"I may be able to help you with that. If you agree, I'll take some measurements and photos of the painting and the diary with my mobile to get a start on the authentication process."

Sadie spoke up: "Why don't you do your work from here, Dean? Remember I have an extra bedroom, so you can work and stay as long as you need."

"I think I'll take you up on your kind offer, Sadie. I'd really like to get started as soon as possible, and the privacy here would be better than the hostel. Also, being here with the painting and diary may help if there are any questions."

Gaston asked, "We have a safe place for the diary, but for now where should we keep the painting?"

"Why don't we just hang it in the sitting room so we can all enjoy it? It's as safe as anywhere. No one knows it's here," answered Dean.

Gaston and Dean hung the painting on a wall in the sitting room, away from any direct sunlight. They were all admiring it when Dean left for the hostel to gather his things. Dean quietly walked out the front door of Sadie's house and climbed into his old rattletrap of a car and slammed the door closed. Laying his head back on the worn seat, he closed his eyes and tried to slow his breath. His heart was pounding so hard and fast, he was worried that even at his young age, he might be having a heart attack—or at the very least, a full-blown panic attack. Out loud, to no one but himself, he whispered, "This will change everything! The Martines will be rich. I'll be famous for discovering a lost masterpiece. My dissertation will be published, and I'll be able to obtain funding to open my gallery!"

He was full of elation and self-satisfaction as he drove back to the hostel.

....

By the next afternoon, though the farm's internet service was slow, Dean was able to determine where, how, and through whom a Van Gogh painting could be authenticated. He learned that Vincent's letters to his brother Theo in 1889, which had later been published, referenced a companion piece to Starry Night called Stormy Day in the Olive Grove. Juliette in her diary had written about Vincent's gift to her of a painting titled Stormy Day in the Olive Grove, and the fact that the painting had been discovered in the home of her family, who had unknowingly possessed it for generations, would go a long way toward proving its provenance. By phone he was assured that the Van Gogh Museum in Amsterdam was the official body for authentication of any of Van Gogh's works. The museum's website touted its state-of-the-art forensic equipment used in the authentication process. He downloaded the museum's application for authentication form and studied it carefully. He felt very sure that he would be completing it very soon and wanted to be ready.

The auction prices he found online for Van Gogh's works were astronomical. This new piece would certainly bring a large hammer price, after it was authenticated.

For the first time, he thought about a commission for his discovery of the diary and the painting, and his continued work in getting them authenticated. He thought a percentage of the hammer price would be appropriate. With this in mind, the outlook for his future instantly changed.

For the first time since his discovery of the painting and the diary, he allowed himself to dream of his future. His truest desire had always been to open an A-list art gallery in one of the world's art centers—New York, London, or Hong Kong. His plan was to represent some of the most prominent artists of the day while cementing his credentials, and later add some of his fellow Sorbonne students and other undiscovered emerging artists.

"If this is truly a Van Gogh, my commission will provide enough money to begin my gallery," he said aloud as he paced the Martines' empty living room. Hearing his words, he realized he needed to discuss such a commission with the Martine family. It had been a long day; he'd sleep on it.

The next morning, he called Gaston and asked him to bring Adrienne and Agnes to Sadie's. He wanted to relay what he had learned. After a long discussion about the authentication process, the need to arrange transportation to Amsterdam, insurance, and other details, it was time to discuss his commission.

"While the ownership of the painting and diary is obviously yours as a family, can I assume you wish to sell both?" asked Dean.

Gaston looked at the rest of the family and answered, "Yes. We would very much like to sell the painting. The money would give us security for the rest of our lives. Security we have never known. We could even help our friends, our church."

"I think that is perfect, Gaston," said Sadie. "But I think we should consider giving Dean Juliette's diary. After all, this is only possible because of him. And maybe some share of the money from the sale of the painting should go to him as well."

This time, Agnes spoke up. "I agree with Sadie. Adrienne and Gaston, do you agree?"

Both nodded yes. "How is this usually arranged, Dean?" asked Adrienne.

36

"First off, I want to thank you for your generous offer to give me Juliette's diary. I am moved beyond words. However, since it is such an important part of the history of this painting, I truly feel it should be sold along with the art. It would increase interest in the sale and most likely result in a much better price than selling them separately." Dean's voice shook with emotion.

He continued, "As for my share of any money from the sale of the painting, from what I've read, this is often done as a percentage of the sales price, usually about a 5 percent commission. Of course, if it is not authenticated, you would owe me nothing."

Gaston reached across the table and took Dean's hand in a firm handshake. "It is done!"

Sadie got out of her chair and walked toward Dean. "It's time for hugs of thanks."

After embracing Sadie, Dean excused himself to make a phone call. Back in Sadie's guest bedroom, he pulled out his mobile, opened his contacts, and dialed a number in Paris.

Art collector Max Bayers recognized the name of the caller on her mobile as the Sorbonne student who had interviewed her for his PhD thesis. Curious, she answered the call. "Hello, Dean. I'm surprised to hear from you again. What can I do for you?"

"Thanks for taking my call, Max. Something truly amazing has happened to me in Arles—I believe I have discovered a fabulous original painting by Van Gogh! But neither the owners nor I have any funds to proceed with authentication. I have strong documentation of its existence from Van Gogh's letters and a diary written by his favorite model that mentions his gift of the painting to her. And it has unknowingly been in her family's hands ever since.

"This could be so huge, Max. But I need your help. I need someone with your experience, expertise, and passion to shepherd this process—and to fund an official authentication at the Van Gogh Museum in Amsterdam, along with expenses like transportation and insurance."

"Dean, give me a minute to collect my thoughts!" she replied.

There was silence on her end before she continued, "If what you think is true, this will be an earth-shattering event in the art world … huge. I'd like to be a part of it, but before I agree, I need some assurance. The first thing is to have someone do an unofficial evaluation, and I know just the man. His name is Peter Meier. He was a world-renowned art expert who was defrocked after being caught denying authentication so a friend could buy an artwork at a low price, and then recanting and authenticating the artwork. His judgment in art is beyond reproach, even though, due to his questionable ethics, no one would now hire him for an official authentication or appraisal. He is readily available, based here in Paris. I am sure I can have him meet you tomorrow in Arles."

"Max, does this mean that if Peter is satisfied that it is a Van Gogh, you will fund the expenses?" asked Dean.

"I'll cover Peter's costs, and as for the rest of the deal, you'll have my answer after we see how Peter responds to the art. But I can say that I am very excited about the possibilities. I'll contact Peter immediately and arrange his travel to Arles to join you. I'll send you the details."

Dean returned to the family in the kitchen with the results of his conversation. "I've just spoken with a wealthy art collector in Paris named Max Bayers. I met her a short time ago while working on my dissertation. She might agree to fund the authentication expenses, but she wants a preliminary evaluation of the painting by an independent appraiser. She recommends Peter Meier and will arrange and pay for his visit here tomorrow."

"This is all overwhelming to us, Dean. We'd be lost without your help," Gaston said.

....

The next morning, Dean collected Peter at the airport in Marseille and drove the eighty kilometers to Sadie's home on the Martine farm. The family was anxiously waiting for them, always eager to enjoy any social interaction. Especially now, since the family's future rested on Peter's evaluation of their painting.

Dean led Peter directly to the painting hanging in the sitting room, with the family following behind. "Oh my!" said Peter as he stood before the painting. "I need more light. Let's take this into the kitchen so I can study it more thoroughly."

Dean carefully removed the painting and led the group into the kitchen, where he placed the painting on the cleared table. Peter stared fixedly at the painting, walking around the table for better views. Twice he rotated the painting to get better light on certain sections. Then he turned it over and looked at the back of the canvas with the title and signature painted on it. He examined the edges of the canvas around the stretcher bars to see the overlap. He then turned the painting right side up and took out a magnifying loop and began to examine the painting in great detail, almost brushstroke by brushstroke. He found the painting to be in excellent condition except for one small area of paint loss in the upper right corner, easily conserved and repaired. During this three-hour process, Dean and the family sat like statues, in total silence.

Finally, Peter straightened up from his bent position and sat down in the single remaining chair. "Thank you for your patience. I truly believe you have an original Van Gogh here. It is wonderful. It is a masterpiece. Once officially authenticated, I feel it should sell at auction for more than €200 million."

Dean bent over, his head in his hands, and exclaimed, "Oh my God! It's real."

The family immediately gathered around Dean, clapping their hands, hugging him and each other, and patting him on the back with pure joy. Then each in turn shook Peter's hand and thanked him gratefully.

Peter responded, "It is my sincere pleasure to give you this news. It is a once-in-a-lifetime moment for me also. Thank you for allowing me to be one of the first to see and the first to evaluate this masterpiece."

"Let's all have a glass of wine to celebrate!" Gaston said as he pulled out a special bottle of wine he had set out earlier in anticipation of this great news.

After he'd had a sip of his wine, Peter apologized and asked to be excused for a moment. "I need to step outside and report to Max in Paris," he explained.

"Max, it's the real thing," he told her when she answered the phone. "I'm sure of it. The painting is in great condition and displays all the characteristics of Van Gogh's paintings. It is as Dean described, a companion piece to Starry Night. The story of this piece will stir the art world," Peter added. "I'll catch a flight from Marseille tonight and see you in Paris in the morning."

"That's fantastic, Peter! Thank you, and please tell Dean that I'll cover the authentication expenses, and I'll expect a 1 percent fee when the sale is completed," Max said before ending the call.

The celebration in the kitchen having finished, Peter said, "I hate to bring this special moment to an end, but Dean, can you drive me back to the airport? I need to get back to Paris."

"Happy to," Dean responded. He then turned to the family, saying, "I'll be back as soon as I can."

....

On his return from the airport, before Dean sat down with the family to talk about next steps, he went directly to his computer. He quickly completed the application form he had saved yesterday from the Van Gogh Museum. He included the information they requested about the discovery of the painting and Juliette's diary along with the photos he had already taken. Now it was time to talk with the family.

"We need to discuss additional financial arrangements. Peter's appraisal gave Max Bayers sufficient confidence that your painting is real, and she has agreed to cover the expenses related to authentication. However, in return, she wants 1 percent of the net sales price of the painting when the art is ultimately sold. That seems reasonable to me, but of course it's up to you. What do you think?" Dean asked.

"We trust your judgment, Dean," Gaston answered as he looked around to the other family members and saw them nodding in agreement.

"Okay that's settled, then. Assuming the Van Gogh Museum will positively respond to the application I just uploaded to them, I'll go ahead and contact Pfyffer and Sons Insurance, the insurance company in Paris recommended by Peter," Dean said as he dialed on his mobile and put it on speaker. After mentioning Peter's name, he was connected directly to James Pfyffer, one of the two sons who now owned the company. After Dean explained the situation, James agreed to transport and insure the art for €10 million, at a cost of €40,000, if the Van Gogh Museum wanted to see the art in person. James was impressed that Peter believed the painting was by Van Gogh and explained that this was why he so readily agreed to offer the contract.

"James, I'm sitting here with the Martines, who own the painting, and they have heard both sides of our conversation. I'm asking, do all of you agree to the insurance company's terms as James has outlined, if the museum does, as I expect, want to see the painting in person?"

"Once again, we all agree," Gaston spoke for the family.

"You heard their agreement, right?" Dean asked James.

"Yes. Let me know as soon as you hear from the authentication board, and I'll have our packers come to Arles and make transportation arrangements. I will overnight an already signed contract to you. Please have all the existing family members sign in front of a notary," said James. "I look forward to hearing from you soon."

As the call ended, Dean turned to the family and said, "All we can do now is wait to hear from the Van Gogh Museum."

....

Dean delayed his return to Paris hoping for a rapid response from the museum. He was rewarded two days later with an early morning call from Maureen Jansen, the secretary of the authentication board at the Van Gogh Museum. She told him that his application had been received and given the highest priority. "Mr. Nixon, it is highly unusual for the board to react with such rapidity, but they would like to see the painting as soon as feasible."

Dean responded, "I have made preliminary arrangements with Pfyffer and Sons to handle crating and shipping. We should be able to have it in your hands within a few days. As soon as final arrangements are confirmed, I will send you the expected delivery details."

Dean ended the call with, "Thank you so very much, Ms. Jansen, for responding so quickly. The family is most grateful for this consideration."

"We look forward to seeing the work, Mr. Nixon."

"This is all moving faster than I could have ever imagined," he said to Sadie as he joined her in the kitchen, where she was preparing breakfast. "The museum just called me, and they want to see the painting. I'll call the insurance company now and see how soon they can transport the painting to Amsterdam."

"This is so exciting, Dean. Go ahead and make the call. I'll keep your breakfast warm," Sadie said with a big smile. "This is really going to happen," she said softly to herself, "maybe I should pinch myself to be sure."

Over breakfast, Dean explained to Sadie, "The insurance company has a van leaving in two days from the Art Institute of Arles going to the Centre Pompidou in Paris for an exhibition of emerging artists. They only have ten unframed pieces they're transporting, so there will be plenty of room in the van for your painting. After delivering the exhibition art in Paris, they'll continue on to Amsterdam. Because of the high value of the insurance, they will send their packers here tomorrow to crate the painting. Their van will pick up your painting the day after tomorrow. They will pick up the other art first, then yours. I'll be leaving for Paris as soon as your crated art is picked up."

....

The entire family surprised him with a special meal his last day at the farmhouse, delaying his departure for Paris. "We want to wish you a safe trip to Paris today. We will anxiously await any word from the museum about the authentication," said Gaston as they all toasted Dean.

"You have my word that I will notify you as soon as I hear anything. May this be the beginning of new lives for all of us!" Dean said as he took a sip of wine.

Chapter 2: A MONTH OF DISCOVERY

Dean arrived at his room in Paris. The drive from Arles and the last few days full of emotional stress had drained his young body of every bit of energy. He dropped onto his lumpy old bed, which felt like a pile of rocks after Sadie's oh-so-soft feather bed, and fell asleep in his clothes. He was dead to the world when his mobile woke him. He rolled over, reached for his mobile, and was surprised to see "Pfyffer and Sons" on the caller ID. Still groggy and not quite awake, he wondered what on earth they could want so early as he answered, "Hello?"

After making sure of Dean's identity, James Pfyffer jumped right to it without so much as a "good morning": "There has been a robbery, and the crate with the Van Gogh is missing."

"What? Wait, who is this?" Dean shook his head, trying to wake.

"I'm James Pfyffer. You arranged for insurance from us for the Van Gogh, for God's sake," James responded irritably. He wanted to get this call over with.

"Yes, yes, I'm sorry. I just woke up. I'm with you now. Tell me what's happening. I just saw it leave the farmhouse yesterday." Dean was incredulous. "How can this be?"

"The local police were at the scene quickly because of the smoke from the fire. It's clear that the other pieces of art in the hijacked van were destroyed in the fire, but the single crate marked for Amsterdam was not there, nor was there any evidence of it being destroyed. It seems clear to the police that it was removed before the van was torched." The Paris police and the arson squad are at a loss.

James kept talking, but his words became a blur. Dean's head only captured some of the more detailed description of the event. The word "torched" sent an icy shiver down Dean's back, in sharp contrast to the sweat that appeared on his face. He heard only words: "hijacked," "gassed," "blood," "missing guard." It was a nightmare. "Wake up, you fool, wake up!" he told himself.

"Be assured, we are sending our own investigators to look into the robbery," James's voice droned on, as if he made this sort of call every day. "Would you be so kind as to notify the Martines of what has happened?" he asked matter-of-factly. Without waiting for a response, he continued, "Of course, we'll let you know the moment we have any other details," and hung up.

"Absolutely. I will talk with them," Dean said before he realized that Pfyffer had ended the call. With growing disbelief, he stared numbly at the phone in his hand.

Dean sat on the edge of his bed, stunned. In one call, everything had changed. All the hopes and dreams they had celebrated yesterday seemed to have evaporated in an instant. What was he to do now? This was all beyond him. He needed advice. He needed help. He needed Max.

"Who's the insurance company?" Max asked as soon as she heard the details from Dean.

"Pfyffer and Sons. Peter recommended them to me," replied Dean.

After a pause, Max volunteered, "My family has a history with Pfyffer. I don't trust them. A piece of treasured art, a Rembrandt portrait that had been in

46

our family for generations, was stolen by the Nazis during the war, then repatriated. Years later, during transport from our home in Paris for an exhibition in Zurich, it was stolen again. The exhibitor assured us that it would be insured. We didn't know the insurance would only cover a small portion of its true value. The contract was with Pfyffer and Sons, who paid off the claim. When it was "found" about three months later in an abandoned warehouse, Pfyffer's contract gave them ownership of our painting for a fraction of its value. I was eventually able to buy it back at its true value of €30 million. I have always believed the theft was an inside job but have never been able to prove it."

She stopped speaking and thought, "I should have followed up with Dean, inquired about the insurance company." She had the beginning of an idea in her head, but it was too early to share it with Dean. "This is about more than money," she thought. It had suddenly become very personal.

"We'll have to let the police complete their investigation first. If they don't get the Van Gogh back, I know what to do next." She didn't wait for Dean to say goodbye, but just ended the call.

After this call, Dean reluctantly made the hardest call of his life, dialing the Martines to tell them about the theft of their painting.

....

The Paris police interviewed Gus, the driver of the art van, in the emergency department of St. Grace Hospital. He was being treated for smoke inhalation and the aftereffects of the unknown gas used by the thieves.

He couldn't give them many details other than the approximate time and location of the hijacking. "I remember a sweet smell when they gassed us. There were two of them and they wore gas masks. Everything happened so fast, I didn't notice anything else about them. I can't even be sure if they were men or women. But where's Joseph? I woke up and he was gone."

The police officer could only respond, "We found some blood on the floor. We're running a DNA analysis, but at this point we don't know where he is. Do you think he could have been involved?"

"I don't know. We went on a lot of runs together, but I don't really know him outside of work. But I'm still worried about him."

....

The forensic team was trying to identify the gas used, but the canisters had been burned with the vehicles. The only clue was Gus's report of a sweet smell. They were working on it. At least the police were able to identify the vehicles. The tow truck had been reported stolen the night before and was of no help. The van was identified as belonging to Pfyffer and Sons Insurance, and they were notified.

The police viewed closed-circuit television footage for the approximate time of the incident in a three-mile radius around the area of suspicion. One of the cameras captured the tow truck and the van. The driver could not be seen clearly; however, his left arm was protruding from the driver's window. When magnified, a partial red coiled-string tattoo could be seen. The police identified this as the symbol of the Red Thread Society, a notorious Chinese triad operating out of one of Paris's two Chinatowns. This possible connection with the gang allowed the police to get a warrant to raid their headquarters. During the raid, they found guns and art listed as stolen, but no Van Gogh. The leader, Chou Bing, and a few of his headmen were arrested.

After a few weeks of dead ends, the police notified Pfyffer and Sons, the Martines, and Dean

Nixon that with no clues, no evidence, and no leads, they now considered the theft a cold case. This meant the case would remain open, but they would no longer actively investigate it unless new evidence appeared. On hearing this, Pfyffer and Sons paid the claim of €10 million to the Martines. Now if the art was ever recovered, it would belong to the insurance company. Dean notified Max with this news.

"What now?" he asked.

"I think it's time for me to speak with the Martines. I have an alternative to giving up," she answered. "I'll pick you up tomorrow at 10:00 AM, and we'll fly down to the Marseille and then drive to Arles so I can present my idea to them in person. You call and set up the meeting for tomorrow afternoon. I'll explain my thoughts to you on the flight down."

"I can't wait to hear what you have to say. Maybe this isn't over yet. At least I hope not," Dean said.

....

In the sitting room of Gaston's house the next afternoon, Max shared her family's troubling history with Pfyffer and Sons and laid out her suspicions and idea.

"I wasn't aware until after the robbery that Pfyffer and Sons was the insuring company. I would have argued against using them. I realize that Dean used Peter, whom I had recommended, as a referral source. So you had every reason to trust him. I am sorry about that. However, as I told Dean, I trust Peter's art knowledge but not his ethical choices. I sincerely believe that Pfyffer and Sons is pulling the same stunt with you that they did with my family. We can't count on the police or Pfyffer's own investigators to help. They have already said there is nothing to find. I am a very wealthy and powerful woman, and I have the means to get to the bottom of this. I hope you'll agree to my plan."

The Martines sat quietly, watching this elegant woman who was so confident in her words, so comfortable taking control of their situation. They hung on her every word in silence, not wanting to interrupt her thoughts.

"There is a very special international team of treasure hunters, based in Singapore, who call themselves Seekers After Lost Treasure, or SALT," Max continued. "They specialize in retrieving valuable lost and stolen works of art. In fact, they recently, on orders of the Pope, retrieved a very important missing chalice related to the Knights Templar and delivered it to the Vatican. I believe I can interest them in your situation, our situation. I believe the insurance company is involved in the theft, and therefore if the art is recovered, it will revert to your ownership. I must warn you that if SALT is able to retrieve the art, they will charge 10 percent of its sale value, but the good news is that if they do not retrieve it, there is no charge. If Pfyffer has nothing to do with the theft, and it is recovered, they will still own the art and you will get nothing, but there will be no cost to you. So you have nothing to lose at this point; you still have the €10 million insurance claim. A lot of money, but nothing like the €100 million or more the painting is worth once authenticated." She paused for a moment to let the Martines process her words. "Would you like me to contact SALT and see if they are interested?"

They all looked to Dean for his response to the question. They all read his silence as an affirmation, and Gaston answered for the family: "We feel like the sheep in our pasture outside. We are wandering. You come from a very different world, Max, even Dean. We hear your words and we try to understand, but in the end, we must trust you both. We're with you, Max, all the way."

"As soon as I can arrange it, I will fly to Singapore and meet with SALT to ask them to take our case." She rose from her chair and approached each member of the family, taking their hands in turn and assuring them, "I will do my very best." Stepping through the door to leave with Dean, she uttered a parting gesture of solidarity: "And so we begin."

JULIETTE'S VAN GOGH

Chapter 3: SINGAPORE

CHALLENGES

Ren Merit, founder of SALT, sat in his office, awaiting the arrival of a former client and friend who needed his help. He had met Max Bayers while he was on assignment to the UN in his twenties. He was working as the Marine liaison to the Task Force for the Repatriation of Stolen Nazi Art. Max had sought help from the task force to recover a Rembrandt that the Nazis had stolen from her family's Paris home during the German occupation.

With a smile, he recalled the first moment he had seen Max Bayers. She had blown into his office at the UN, a young ball of energy. She seemed to arrive with a tailwind—a strikingly tall, willowy brunette, about his own age, who he would soon learn was as brilliant and accomplished as she was stunning.

Ren had been instrumental in successfully recovering the family's Rembrandt, but he had lost touch with her in the years since and was anticipating her arrival with great curiosity. In those years, she had expanded her family's successful business and had become a wildly successful mogul in the world of high tech. He had recently seen her name in Forbes's list of billionaires.

Alfredo Embroli, a dapper Italian and SALT's facility manager and occasional chauffer and chef, interrupted Ren's thoughts and ushered Max into his office.

"Max, it's been a few years. Welcome to SALT," Ren warmly greeted her, taking her hands in his.

"It's good to see you, Ren," she said. "I really appreciate your arranging to see me so quickly, for responding to my call for help."

"Have a seat and tell me what's going on. Tell me about this missing piece of art."

Max and Ren settled in as she began to share the details about the discovery of the long-lost Van Gogh, its theft, and her involvement. Ren, dressed in his usual black shirt and cargo pants, which flattered his long-fit frame, looked at Max and smiled, remembering how very much he had enjoyed her company in the past. Seated in his other armchair, she looked relaxed, rested, and casually elegant even after her long flight to Singapore in her private jet. But, being the Max he had known, she was all business and wanted to get to it, to share her story with him.

To explain her passion and urgency about this assignment, Max first brought Ren up to date about the second theft of her family's masterpiece—the very painting he had helped recover earlier for her.

"Ren, I believed something was very wrong. I was suspicious that Pfyffer had stolen our art, but I had no proof. And now I am involved with this Van Gogh deal. It's been stolen, and I see the same thing in motion again. I want to get these bastards, and my contacts tell me your team is my best chance."

"I've made the Martines and Dean aware of your 10 percent commission. I previously agreed to finance the authentication process for the Martines for a percentage of the painting's sale. However, if there is a recovery and the insurance company is not proved to be involved with the theft, the insurance company will continue to own the painting. The Martines will have no claim to the painting, and there will be no commission. You could petition the insurance company for a finder's fee, but they would have no legal obligation to pay you."

"I'm sure you also know that if the art is not recovered, there would be no commission," Ren added. "That's our promise to our clients."

"I know the risk of SALT not collecting any fees is high. At present, there is little evidence and few clues, so this assignment is largely based on my suspicions. But if you agree, I will cover all your expenses if you receive no commission, so you're only risking your time for a potentially large payoff." Shifting to the front of her seat to move closer to Ren, she handed him a thin stack of files she had pulled from her leather portfolio. "As you'll see from these police reports, there was a possible clue related to the Red Thread Society, but it turned out to be a false lead."

"Did the insurance company use their own investigators?" Ren asked.

"Yes, they did, and it is all here. Everything is here: the Red Thread Society report and all the other reports and interviews. There are also some minimal notes from Pfyffer and Sons. I don't think they put much effort into it, which increases my suspicion and desire for vengeance," she said in a tone of disgust.

"I obviously need to give this some thought. I need to review these reports and get my field team involved. Then we'll be able to make a decision together. We really do work as a team, especially since a previous high-value case put our lives in danger. I want unanimity before agreeing on all high-value assignments because of the potential risk. Their lives could be on the line again. I'll set up a meeting with the team for this afternoon to share this information. We'll make a decision tomorrow morning. Is that satisfactory to you?"

"Of course. I'd expect nothing less from you. You certainly wouldn't make an impulsive decision. I have some other business here in Singapore that will keep me busy. How about dinner tonight so we can catch up on old times?" she asked.

He agreed enthusiastically. "Why don't I have Alfredo prepare dinner for us here? We can talk without the noise and the risk of being overheard in a public place. How about 7:00?"

"Perfect. I'm at the Fullerton, always my parents' favorite. I'll take their Rolls back here," she said as they rose and hugged. "Thank you, Ren."

Ren spent the next two hours going over the reports in detail, including the CCTV photograph with the partial tattoo showing. "This was a well-organized and orchestrated heist," he thought. "The biggest puzzle is how the thieves knew when and where the art van would or could be found. I wonder if there was a tracking device on the art or the van, like the sophisticated micro-GPS trackers used to track us in the hunt for the chalice. There seem to be few clues and a truckload of suspects. I'd better start on a list that we can all add to, so that no one gets left out." He then set up a meeting with the field team.

....

That afternoon, Ren gathered his team together in the sleek modern conference room at Central, as they referred to their quiet villa on the outskirts of Singapore. It was an idyllic oasis, its gardens' flowering blooms designed to ensure that the fragrance of jasmine and a host of other pleasant scents greeted them each day. The entire staff enjoyed living and working at Central, as it was peppered with art everywhere. Sometimes they recovered an artwork for a client who could not afford to pay the 10 percent fee, and they were given fabulous art in exchange. The villa was elaborately armed with state-of-the-art security to protect this valuable art collection.

One by one, they arrived and took their usual seats around the table. Ren was always amused that each time they met, everyone chose exactly the same piece of real estate. Alexandria Nussa, or Alex, the ex-Seabee with her ponytail bobbing, the team's fixer of all things electromechanical, was the first to take her seat. Next was Kat Dubois, an exotic-looking Eurasian who loved sleek, stylish fashions. With her profound mathematical and analytical mind, she had become SALT's main problem solver and Ren's trusted confidant. As always, she took her seat next to Alex. Harley and Drew were the last to arrive. Harley Bechman, resident expert in Krav Maga, the highly effective self-defense system developed by the Israeli military, was charged with maintaining SALT's safety and security and directing logistics. His trim and fit physique fitted perfectly into his usual slim jeans and polo shirt. He set his coffee cup on the table and sat down opposite Alex. Drew Saul, SALT's chief information officer, slid into his chair at the table dressed in a white shirt and colorful bow tie. Always the one left home at Central, Drew was responsible for SALT's research needs, especially when the team was in the field.

Maria Pappas, their Greek housekeeper and assistant cook, delivered their beverages of choice. She knew exactly what each would order and never, ever delivered any alcohol to Harley. He was over ten years sober and a determined member of AA.

"You all know by now that Max Bayers was here to meet with me this morning," Ren began. "She is an old friend from my UN days, and she wants our help."

He quickly filled them in on his history with Max, the Nazis' theft of her family's Rembrandt, its repatriation, and its more recent theft. Then he detailed

Max's experience with Pfyffer and Sons Insurance and her suspicions surrounding the Rembrandt's more recent theft and her repurchase of the artwork at full value.

"Now there has been a Van Gogh stolen associated with the same insurance company. This explains why she is so emotionally involved in this case. She feels this is a pattern she wants very much to expose and stop. And she seeks revenge!" he added.

"This is another fascinating case, guys," he continued, leaning forward in his seat and opening the file before him. He smiled at his team. "Do we really ever get any that aren't?"

"That's why we all love this gig, right?" Alex responded with a big grin as she took a sip of her cold drink. Everyone else piled on with their own quips, which let the team know they felt exactly the same way.

Ren recounted all the information that Max had given him about the Van Gogh, laying it out for the team in his usual storybook but methodical manner, which always had them hanging on his every word. They had often told him that he should be writing mystery novels instead of running around the world solving other people's mysteries. His stock answer was "And miss out on all the adventure with you guys?"

The team sat fascinated by the tale of the once-in-a-lifetime discovery of an unknown masterpiece and its swift theft. It set their adrenaline levels racing; this was the stuff they all lived for. They would all readily admit that they were adrenaline junkies.

"Our potential payoff for this job, if we take it, has a twist," Ren told them, slowly closing the file in front of him. "The ownership of the painting, if it is recovered, will reside with Pfyffer and Sons Insurance, per their contract with the Martines, since they have paid the insurance claim. In this scenario, if we recover the painting and the insurance company is not involved in the theft, we will get no commission. Because of this risk, Max will cover our expenses if we do not end up with a commission. I think this is very generous of her. If, however, the insurance company is found guilty of the theft and the associated fraud, the ownership will revert to the Martines. If that happens, we will get our usual commission. The Martines have already agreed to this. Thoughts or questions at this point?"

Harley quickly spoke up: "Does this twist remind anybody but me of our last assignment, when we were searching for a chalice that no one could even prove beyond a doubt actually existed? This case seems to have our MO on it. There are lots of unknowns—starting with, is it really a Van Gogh? We also have a client with multiple motives. Let's not allow her thirst for vengeance to color our thinking."

"I get your point," Kat responded. "We all need to spend some time reviewing what we have in hand, from each of our own perspectives … as always."

"Absolutely, and to help get you started, I'd like each of you to review this information, including the police and insurance company reports." Ren passed thin files to each of the team. "Please keep in mind that the van's security guard is still missing, and his blood was found at the scene. Victim or culprit, we don't know. This may be a signal of potential danger in this mission.

"Also, you'll see that I've prepared a list of potential suspects, which you will recognize from the history I just gave you." Looking at his notes, Ren read the list aloud. "Drew, I'd like you to begin preliminary background checks on the people I have on this list as well as anyone else you uncover in reviewing the material. Let's meet tomorrow morning at 9:00 to make a final decision on this assignment. Thanks, everybody."

"Drew ..." Pulling him aside, Ren asked, "Before you leave, would you give me a minute?"

"Of course," Drew answered as the rest of the team gathered up their papers and left the conference room.

Once the conference room was empty, Ren said, "Can you give me an update on the Rose Stern case? And some idea of how Shiloh's working out. I need to know if it was the right move to send her back here to work with us ... in fact, work with you."

"Well, we settled her in a safe house as soon as she arrived from Paris. She dug right in on the project. I think it helped her a lot to have something to focus on. As a matter of fact, she is flying to Prague tomorrow on a lead. I've been handling the details myself since you called from Paris and explained the situation. So far, both Shiloh and I have spoken to Rose Stern several times. This has been especially hard on her, losing the Claude Lorrain painting a second time. First by the Nazis, which you helped repatriate, and now this latest theft. We've just learned that its value has risen to €10 million at auction. It has been an unbelievable tragedy for Rose, especially at her age. Shiloh has been very good with her, putting her at ease—especially when she relayed that you wouldn't be active on the case this time. Your chance meeting at the de Gaulle airport after ten years was meaningful for Rose. I think she was hopeful that you'd personally help her again."

"I'm sure it's a disappointment." Ren had grown close to this now elderly client years ago and understood her response to the circumstances. "I'll call her very soon and assure her that I am never completely out of the picture and she can reach out to me at any time."

"Thanks, Ren, I think that would help a lot."

Shifting his body a bit, Drew changed the tone of the conversation. "Shiloh's made contact with a longtime art collector that she knew from her work as a curator. He lives in Prague and told her about a local dealer there who has a black-market Lorrain for sale. Apparently, this dealer's father was aligned with the Nazis' 'art program' of plunder by theft and coercively cheap sales of masterpieces of Jewish-owned art during the war. Somehow, he escaped punishment and now his son has a contemporary gallery in Prague. He works with mostly emerging young European artists. With his past family connections, he is also rumored to have an illicit private collection of old masterpieces from his father's Nazi days and more from recent thefts, all of which he sells to special private collectors.

"This Prague collector says he will introduce Shiloh to this dealer and vouch for her so she can see his cache of stolen art. The collector has great bona fides and is known to Shiloh. She has agreed to fly to Prague to see if the Lorrain is there. To be sure of her safety, as you've asked, Harley has arranged for a respected security firm in Prague to provide bodyguard services for her. The owner is an old friend of Harley's from his Mossad days."

Drew paused and then sighed. "She asks about you, Ren. It's been hard. I never know quite what to say to her about you."

"I don't know either, Drew." Ren turned away from Drew and started to slowly make his way toward the conference room door, Drew following at his heels. "So sorry to put you in this situation. It's not been fair to either of you. I just need some time, some space to work through my feelings about her. Trust is a hard one. It comes before your heart's desires, or at least we're taught it should." Shaking his head to clear his thoughts, Ren stopped and faced Drew. "Sorry again, Drew. And thanks for arranging for the security for her. I'll thank Harley also. I don't want anything to happen to her, no matter what our relationship becomes."

"Understood." Drew laid his hand for a brief moment on Ren's arm in a gesture of support. "I'll get started on the background checks, and I'll let Shiloh know that her plan for Prague is a go. I'll also be checking in with her daily."

"Thanks, Drew," Ren said softly as Drew turned and left the conference room.

....

That evening, Max and Ren were seated at a small table in Ren's private office, as Alfredo had decided that this was a better, more intimate place for the two to have a private dinner than the much larger conference/dining room. He thought at first to prepare cuisses de grenouille, but he knew some people didn't like the idea of sautéed frog legs. He knew for certain that it wasn't one of Ren's favorites. For a starter, he'd settled on a Camembert fondue with pieces of French baguette for dipping. He had turned the lights low to set off Ren's art treasures, which were carefully arranged on the walls and tables in his office.

Their first wine was a Louis Latour Puligny-Montrachet 2016, a wine Ren had just discovered while working on the Templars' chalice case in Burgundy. Ren lifted his wineglass and proposed a toast, "To reunions."

"To reunions indeed, my friend." Max lifted her glass to his. "This is quite a world you've created here in the middle of Singapore—a long way from Oxford, the Marines, the UN. It appears you've had an interesting journey," she added, gesturing with her wineglass to the art and relics in the room.

"As have you, it would seem," Ren responded. "You've become a world-class art collector, and in quite a different league from me, I understand. And you've done it through your own hard work and colossal successes."

"My parents' fortune gave me a large platform to launch my tech ventures, but it's true I've taken it all to sometimes breathtaking heights. It's been a rush, a thrill ride full of challenges, battles both lost and won."

"Any regrets?" asked Ren.

"Well, I'm looking at one."

Ren almost choked on his last sip of wine. "Did I miss something?"

"Well, I've had the feeling more than once over the last years that I did … miss something, that is," she said with a bit of a smile. "I was this ambitious young thing in New York meeting this lanky Oxford-educated Marine who also loved art. I was too cool by far to see what was right in front of me. Or I was too cool to acknowledge to myself what I felt about him at the time. Now I seem to have everything I've ever wanted, but looking at you, I think maybe not. We make choices in our lives, Ren. You and I live in fast lanes … different lanes, but fast to be sure. It's easy to let time slip away—an old cliché, but a true one."

"Interesting that you should say that, Max. I've been wrestling with a very important choice in my life for the last several weeks, and it all comes down to trust. Trusting myself and trusting her. I've never felt more unsure of my judgment, my feelings, my future."

Alfredo interrupted just then to bring in the next course, clear the first course away, and introduce the next wine.

"The Camembert fondue was luscious," Max told Alfredo, speaking from her vast culinary experience as she dipped her last bit of crusty bread into the fondue. "The drizzle of honey and olive oil over the rosemary and thyme made it so much better."

As Alfredo removed the plates from the fondue course, he thanked Max for her kind kudos. "The next course is a pumpkin charcoal ravioli, a specialty of Singapore, with chickpeas, red onion, balsamic vinegar, and importantly, black truffles. I'll be pouring another burgundy Ren just shipped home from France. It's a 2012 Gevrey-Chambertin, a beautiful pinot noir."

"Watch out, Ren, I may try to steal him away …
I have a lovely villa in the Piedmont that Alfredo might
enjoy making his home base," mused Max over her
delectable ravioli.

"Most kind of you, Max, but I'm very much at
home here at Central," Alfredo said with clear pride of
belonging and sense of ownership.

"Be warned, Alfredo, I almost never take no for
an answer." Max smiled as she took a sip of the lovely
pinot.

Dessert consisted of a lavender honey-baked
muscat melon tarte tatin with grated lemon and orange
in phyllo pastry. As Alfredo served it with an old chilled
Madeira muscat wine from Central's wine cellar, Max
returned to their earlier conversation. "Ren, can I
intrude on your private world for a moment?"

Ren responded with a, "where's this going?"
look on his face but said, "Okay …"

"I made a choice many years ago about you,
and yes, I do indeed regret it. May I say as one who
has struggled with personal choice … if she—"

Ren offered, "Shiloh. Shiloh Pritizi."

"—if Shiloh has this hold on your heart, your
mind … you owe it to yourself, and perhaps to her, to
find out where this path can take you. You've been a
risk taker all your life, Ren, as have I. Emotional risks
terrify people like us. Take the next step. It may turn
out to be a step off a cliff, or it may turn out to be the
best, most rewarding, and important risk of your life."
Max felt tears stinging her eyes, her words surprising
even herself. She lifted her glass of wine to distract
Ren from seeing the depth of her feelings, but she
failed.

"Thank you, Max. There's probably no one else
in the world who could or would share those thoughts
with me and make me feel and believe everything
that's behind each word. I'm thankful and honored by
your honesty."

After coffee and Armagnac, Ren walked Max to her waiting Rolls for her ride back to her hotel. "Thank you for tonight, Ren. I'll never forget it," she said as she reached up and gave him a hug. She whispered in his ear, even though there was no one to hear, "Yes, you were and always will be my one regret. Don't make my mistake, Ren, you deserve better ... much better."

Before he could respond, she had slipped into the back seat of the waiting car and was gone. He stood there for a few minutes in the heat of the Singapore evening and then reached for his mobile.

"If it's not too late, I need to see you ... tonight."

....

Ren drove toward the safe house that SALT used when they wanted someone out of harm's way but not at Central. It had been two weeks since the team's return from Paris and the close of the Vatican assignment. He had flown Shiloh to Singapore after she'd admitted that when they'd first met in Paris, she had been sent by her boss to find out what the team's travel plans were. She was unaware that with this information, she would be putting Ren and his team in danger. But at that first meeting, something had happened between them that had changed everything.

Their dinner together a few nights later confirmed for Ren that the feelings he had for this extraordinary woman were feelings that he had never experienced before. These feelings both scared and confused him. He and Shiloh met again in Milan four days later, when Ren arrived as part of the search for the missing Templars' Chalice. It was here that Shiloh admitted that she had met him the first time under false pretenses, which had crushed Ren's soul. Shiloh told him that ever since that night, she had refused to help her boss, Hans Rhinehardt, by gathering any information on Ren. Hans had immediately fired her as curator of his private museum in Germany.

Ren hadn't known what to do about his feelings of hurt, perhaps love, and at the same time mistrust and anger. He only knew that he had to protect her from this very violent and dangerous man. And so he had asked Drew to book her a flight to Singapore, provide her with a safe place, and let her work on the Rose Stern project until he could figure out where he was in his own head and heart. Since returning to Singapore two weeks ago, Ren had avoided any contact with Shiloh. Max's words tonight made him realize that he had to move on and quit running away from his emotions.

Ren arrived at the safe house and walked quickly to the door.

Shiloh had been packing for her flight to Prague the next day. She put one more piece of clothing into her suitcase and then dropped down on her bed in tears. Was he coming to say goodbye? She prayed not … she prayed for a miracle. But her life so far hadn't had any miracles, except for one, meeting Ren.

Hearing the doorbell, Shiloh slowly rose and answered the door. She was dressed in sweats, her blond hair tied at the nape of her neck with a piece of ribbon. Ren's call after so much silence had left her trembling.

Ren could see that Shiloh had been crying and he suspected that he was the reason. All the words he'd thought to say on the way over evaporated. He stepped into the room and took Shiloh into his arms. She melted against him with a sob. He held her weight to keep her from collapsing. He buried his face in her neck and for the first time since childhood, felt the relief of tears run down his cheeks. They stood holding each other, neither speaking, just feeling, just letting out all the tensions of the last weeks.

At last Shiloh pulled her head back and looked into Ren's face, "I …"

Ren stopped her next word and kissed her … and kissed her … and kissed her. And she returned each of his kisses with her own. Finally they pulled a bit apart. Winded as if he had just stepped over the finish line in a sprint, Ren asked, "Can we sit and talk?"

Shiloh took his hand and lead him to the small sofa in the living room, answering, "Please … there's so much I want to say."

As they sat down Shiloh positioned herself facing him and Ren gently took her into his arms. She loved him holding her and nestled her head into the crook of his neck. "There's so much I want to say to you too," Ren said softly. "To start with, I'm so sorry for my distance, my silence, my fear."

Shiloh lifted her head to look him in the face. "I understood, but I prayed every day that you'd find a way to forgive me, to give me a chance to show you who I am, to see me free of the mistake I made that put you and your team in danger. But, I also was terrified that it might never be possible."

"An old friend told me tonight that she regretted letting someone she had cared for slip away while she was consumed with her ambition, her life on the fast track, and she warned me not to make the same mistake. She encouraged me to take a risk, to reach out to you and put my heart on the line with no guarantees—because there never are any in life—and not to turn my back on this opportunity for love." Taking Shiloh's face in his hands, he asked, "Can you do that with me, Shiloh? Can you take a chance on me? Can we try this together and see where it takes us, no guarantees?"

"A chance, Ren, that's all I ask for too—a chance to see what this is, where it takes us. But I know I love you. I knew it that night over dinner in Paris."

"If I'm honest with my heart, I think that I knew it then too, Shiloh. It was such a new feeling to me, I didn't have the words. I've been so busy with my life that a part of me hasn't been living, if that makes sense to you at all. It sounds so crazy, but it's what I've been feeling since we met."

Shiloh slowly sat up and faced Ren. "Can I show you how I feel about you?" she whispered softly as she deliberately pulled the ribbon from her hair and let her hair fall down around her face. "No more words, just feelings?" She stood, taking his hands in hers. "Will you come with me and let us trust each other with our bodies? Just trust, and be free of any fears and doubts, and see where it leaves us on the other side?"

Ren stood up and carefully lifted her off the floor into his arms. He kissed her tenderly and carried her into the bedroom, answering softly, "I love you, Shiloh."

Chapter 4: COMMITMENT

The next morning at 9:00 sharp, Ren quieted the room and said, "Let's get to it. As always, our decision on this assignment must be unanimous or we won't take it. On its face, it doesn't appear particularly dangerous, but with its high value, more than €200 million for such a Van Gogh, it could become so at any point. Remember our last assignment for the Vatican? It looked safe at first, but it put us in mortal danger. And remember that the guard is missing—dead or alive, we don't know. We've all had overnight to think about it. Do you have a decision?"

Kat, who had been severely wounded in a terrifying knife attack on the last mission, sat forward in her chair, her back rigid as if at attention in a military exercise. "I'm speaking for all of us, since I was the one who had to come back to Central early because of my injuries. We all have discussed this at length, both last night and again at breakfast, and we all have agreed that the reward for achieving success on this assignment is worth the potential risk."

After a short pause, Ren broke out in a pleased smile; his team had come through for him once again. "Then it's a go! I thank you for your courage, always, and for putting your hearts and souls into our SALT ventures. May this one lead to good and great things for all of us." They all broke out in a self-congratulatory round of applause.

"Okay, let's jump right in. I want all of you to study my list of possible suspects again and make sure I didn't leave anyone off. I have special tasks for each of you. Kat, you and Alex look into who may be looking for a Van Gogh to fill in their collection, even if it is stolen. I think we can forget about Hans Rhinehardt, since his henchmen are in jail and he is under an Interpol microscope since the fiasco with the chalice. But there are others. Be sure to check out social media for any rumors.

"Drew, you're already working on the background checks. Be sure to look closely into Pfyffer and Sons, as Max feels strongly that they are involved. It could have been anyone at the insurance company, whether the owners or someone who knew about the Van Gogh and wanted it for themselves, whether to sell on the black market or keep, or to use to discredit the company. Check the owners' and principals' finances, look at their bank accounts. They probably have numbered ones. Use your contacts and try to find any offshore accounts.

"So, we're headed back to Paris. Harley, book air reservations for tomorrow evening and hotel reservations again at the Hotel Pyramide.

"I'll call Max and give her the good news and let her know that we'll be in Paris soon. We'll meet at 9:00 AM tomorrow to see what progress we've made.

"On a personal note, before you leave, I want to thank you for being patient with me the last couple of weeks, knowing I've been going through a difficult time about Shiloh. I want to be open with you. The truth is, we're in love with each other. There are no guarantees, but as of last night, it's our beginning. You are my family, and I wanted—I needed—to share this news with you. Thank you."

The team spontaneously greeted him with hoots of "It's about time!" and "What took you so long?" and erupted once more into a spontaneous and rowdy round of applause. They were all grinning from ear to ear as each in turn hugged Ren as they left the room.

....

The team reassembled in the conference room the following morning at 9:00 on the dot. "Now comes the hard part. Where do we go from here?" Ren asked.

Kat, whose grasp of disparate information made her an invaluable second-in-command to Ren, said, "Let's look at the usual parameters: motive, means, and opportunity. It appears greed or money is the most likely, though we can't rule out the possibility of love and jealousy or revenge. Let's look at all the potential players.

"I'll start with a couple of unlikely but easy ones," she continued. "First, there is Dean Nixon. Maybe he wants the painting for himself, or to sell it on the black market. But why not just buy the painting from the owners for a nominal amount and then 'discover' that it's an original Van Gogh later? Maybe in his enthusiasm he spoke up about its being a Van Gogh without thinking it through. Also, there are the artists who did not get accepted into the Pompidou exhibition. Maybe one of them was jealous and decided to hijack the van and destroy all the paintings without being aware that a Van Gogh was among them. Or anyone working at the Pompidou who might have known about the Van Gogh and the shipping schedule. All of them are suspects but unlikely. I think we should focus on the more likely scenarios."

"Another far-out possibility," Drew said, "is narcotraffickers. I have found references on the dark web that some have begun to use art as currency. It is much easier to carry, hide, or transport a painting than a huge stack of cash or gold. Diamonds worked for a while, but now with all the notoriety of 'blood diamonds,' they are getting harder to maneuver. Usually, however, art is used that has a documented value, such as an auction price. This unauthenticated

Van Gogh doesn't fit that profile. But you must admit that carrying a €100 million painting rolled up in a piece of PVC pipe is easier than trying to hide the same amount of gold, about 6,000 pounds worth, or a huge flatbed of cash. I would suggest that if our investigations point toward narcotraffickers, we abandon the search. They are too ruthless and too well armed for us to be successful and survive."

Alex timed her comments just right, while everyone was mulling over motives for stealing the Van Gogh. "We have to consider that an unknown collector may have orchestrated the theft on demand and that the painting is now well hidden in some secret cache of art. If this is so, the probability of finding it is very slim. So I think we should focus on the more likely thieves."

"And just who do you think those are?" Kat quizzed as she got out of her chair to stretch her healing leg.

"Well, it seems to me there are a couple with the means, opportunity, and motive to pull off such a heist," Alex continued. "There remains the Red Thread Society. Just because the painting was not found doesn't mean they didn't steal it. Or another gang, stealing it for the money and at the same time implicating the Red Thread Society, for a variety of reasons. There could be a turf war, jealousy, or just revenge for some reason. The other two groups include the insurance company itself or someone in its ranks, out to make a killing with inside information. And lastly don't forget the authentication board at the Van Gogh Museum in Amsterdam or someone associated with it."

It was quiet for a few moments as they all thought over these possibilities. Finally Ren spoke up. "Drew, what did you find out about the triads?"

His trademark bow tie bobbing up and down as he referenced his iPad, Drew explained, "Centuries ago in China, a few groups or societies were set up to provide help and support for specific clans and families. A sort of benevolent society. Over time, some became involved in criminal activities. Eventually Mao drove many of them out of China, but they still exist today, in China and in other countries.

"As you're all well aware, Chinatowns exist in most large cities of the world. Generations of Chinese immigrants live, work, and die there, many retaining their original language, dialects, customs, and culture. Though many triads provide social assistance and are benign, others are criminal and focus on illegal drugs, human trafficking, protection scams, money laundering, and loan sharking. These latter triads have a very militaristic structure with absolute obedience required. They can be very aggressive with anyone betraying their secrets, yet to some extent they do provide a safe neighborhood … as long as everyone pays up. These triads continue to prey on the Chinese and other immigrants and often go to war to enlarge their domain, not only against other triads but also against the Russian and Italian mafias.

"With this in mind, I reexamined the CCTV photo of the tattoo. It didn't look quite right to me. So I asked Aurora, a forensic scientist whom I recently added to our elite cadre of resources, to examine it. Indeed, the red thread in the tattoo was coiled in a different direction than the Red Thread Society symbol. Further, the color was not as pure a red. It had some brown in it, and Aurora suggested it was a henna tattoo, as the natural dye used in henna tattoos is a reddish brown. Since henna is superficial on the skin and fades in a couple of weeks, it makes a good temporary tattoo. In contrast, a regular tattoo penetrates the skin's dermis and is permanent. So it appears this tattoo was a red herring.

"Getting back to the triads, there are two big triads in Paris. One is in the Belleville neighborhood, the Red Thread Society. The other is in the

Olympiades Chinatown. The triad running this area is extremely secretive. It doesn't even have an official or legitimate business outlet, as the Red Thread Society does. It has been given the nickname of the Ghost Triad.

"I believe the thieves knew where the CCTV camera was and provided this false lead to either throw suspicion off of them and or to discredit the Red Thread Society, making it easier to move into their territory. So, if a triad is involved, it could be a competitor to the Red Thread Society. The only one I could identify as a possibility was the Ghost Triad. They do seem to be ghosts, as they come and go at leisure, and no one has been able to infiltrate or turn a member. This triad appears to be behind many criminal activities, but no one can identify an actual member. Their nickname seems very apt to me."

"Thank you, Drew," said Ren. "We have so much ground to cover, I suggest we split up into two teams. Kat, you and Harley go to Arles and talk with the director of the Art Institute. Obtain a list of the artists who submitted art for the Pompidou exhibition and focus on those who were rejected. Interview them, as well as anyone else who might have known the transport schedule and route. See if you can determine if any had a strong motive, if they had alibis, and if any had the financial means or contacts to carry out the hijacking for them.

"Once that is accomplished, head for Amsterdam and investigate the Van Gogh Museum's authentication board and anyone connected with the board, or with the museum, who may have known the van's schedule and have any possible motives."

"Got it." Kat added notes to her mobile. "I'll make appointments for the Art Institute of Arles and the Van Gogh Museum in Amsterdam."

Harley chimed in, "And I'll make all the travel arrangements for Kat and myself."

"I'll set up a meeting with Detective Arnot, the lead investigator in charge of the theft, for Alex and me," Ren said, "while you two are on your way to Arles. We have the police reports, but I want to see if anything new has come up or if there are any lingering unanswered feelings or intuitions about the case. Sometimes these gut feelings are as good as clues but don't get in the report because there's no actual evidence. Also, we'll check with the gang task force and see what we can find out about these triads. Maybe they have made some inroads or have informants whose connections we might tap into."

Alex looked at Ren quizzically and said, "I thought the Red Thread Society was exonerated."

"No, just because they didn't find the Van Gogh in the police raid doesn't mean the triad is innocent. We need to make our own decisions about that. The fake tattoo may have been planted to first suggest they were the culprits and then to exonerate them when the tattoo was discovered to be a fake. If so, a very clever plan," Ren said. "It got them off the police suspect list, though some members and the leader are in jail for possession of stolen artworks and illegal weapons. So, maybe not so clever.

"Alex, after we meet with Detective Arnot, you and I will go to Pfyffer and Sons Insurance Company, and then to the Pompidou to talk with the curator of the exhibit. Then the next day we'll pay a surprise visit to Peter Meier, since Max is so sure the insurance company is tied up with the theft and Peter is the link to them. Afterward, we'll go to see Dean Nixon at his flat. I want us to see him in his normal environment, see how he lives. We'll feel him out about possible motives, his alibi, get a list of his friends who may have known about the Van Gogh discovery and investigate them.

"Let's all email the names of any suspects we can't rule out to Drew so he can do a deeper investigation. We want any criminal associations, gang-related information, personal financial situations, etc. We'll have a conference call every evening at 8:00 PM Paris time. That means it will be 3:00 AM the next day in Singapore for you, Drew. Sorry," Ren said. He sat quietly for a few moments as if he had just run out of steam.

Harley broke the silence. "I have booked overnight flights on Singapore Air, and you and Alex are booked at the Pyramide. I alerted the hotel that your two-bedroom suite needs to be ready by 6:00 AM, when our overnight flight arrives. That way you'll have a chance to catch a couple of hours' sleep before your appointment with Detective Arnot at the police station. Kat and I will continue on to Arles."

PRAGUE – SHILOH'S CHALLENGE

On arrival in Prague, Shiloh emailed a message to Drew as promised:

Hi Drew,

Reporting in. Just arrived in Prague and have checked in to the Grand Citadel. Very nice, thank you. I could get accustomed to being spoiled like this! And I love that it's near the art district. They mentioned it when I checked in. My main security guys are Jakup and Adam. As you arranged, they're staying in the hotel in the room adjacent to mine; in fact, they have a connecting door, so I feel very safe. They explained that they'll be taking twelve-hour shifts with backups for their time off.

I've already placed a call to my collector friend Milos, and he has informed me that Gustaf—our dealer/suspect—is unavailable for the next two days. Milos arranged an appointment for us to meet him at his legitimate gallery in the city in three days. Milos is convinced that Gustaf has the work we're looking for, based on the photo I sent him from Singapore. So, we'll see.

I guess I'll be doing some touring with Jakup for the next few days. It's good to be out of the Singapore condo. But wouldn't it be lovely if Ren was here with me? I'm thinking out loud, Drew, please ignore.

Anyway, signing off. Thinking that text and email are probably the easiest and most efficient way to communicate with you for now.

Over and out,
Shiloh

P.S. I'll be using the name Anna Peak with Gustaf just in case he knows

Hans. I'll explain to Milos since he knows me as Shiloh.

Chapter 5: DAY ONE

PARIS

The next day, Ren and Alex arrived at the Paris Central Police Station promptly at 10:00 AM. Ren introduced himself to the desk sergeant. "We've an appointment with Detective Arnot."

They were directed into a small office at the end of a musty hall. The office was very sparse, with just a metal desk and a couple of chairs. There was nothing on the walls, and the stagnant air held the distinct smell of old Gauloises cigarettes and stale coffee. After introductions and the sharing of business cards, Detective Arnot offered them a seat. The untidiness of the office caused Ren to wonder how the detective could ever keep anything straight.

Detective Arnot was at least thirty pounds overweight, balding, and somewhat curt. "What can I do for you?" he asked in almost unaccented English.

"My team from Singapore is investigating the art van hijacking and theft of a supposed Van Gogh some weeks ago. We've read your reports. They were very informative and complete. We know you spent considerable time and effort to solve the crime. However, I know from past experience that sometimes police investigators have a feeling about a case. A sense that something isn't right, an intuition or hunch, which doesn't make it into the official report, since only determined facts are reported. Did you or any of the other investigators have a sense of who was involved even though there was no concrete evidence?"

"No, I'm sorry, but we had no inkling of who may have been involved. And believe me, we looked. The potential high value of this crime got all of us looking under every rock. I don't have much to offer you in any case.

"The only new thing since the reports is that the forensic team has matched the blood found in the rear of the warehouse with that of the missing guard, Joseph Boucher. His blood was on record from the time he spent in the army. We found nothing to believe he was involved, leading us to conclude he was a victim. Where he is now, and whether he is alive or dead, we don't know.

"As you know from reading our reports, our one good lead was the Red Thread Society, a local Chinese triad. A raid on their facilities led to some stolen art, though none from the hijacking, and some illegal weapons. This led to some arrests, but we did not find the Van Gogh. They vehemently denied being involved, though of course we didn't take their plea of innocence seriously. We have no further leads."

"No hunches or hints as to who was behind this?" Ren asked one more time to be very sure.

"No, I don't have any, and none of my officers mentioned anything they thought was out of the ordinary. Sorry I can't help you more."

Alex leaned forward despite the strong odor of cigarettes and coffee on Detective Arnot's breath and said, "I think I sense that there's a lingering suspicion that the Red Thread Society is involved despite their disclaimers and no Van Gogh found."

"Maybe so, but with no further evidence, the case has been filed as a cold case."

"Is there any way we could talk with their current leader—not the jailed Chou Bing, but the person who's taken over?" asked Alex.

"I assume you know this is a very dangerous gang, but we do have an informant planted at the fringes of the group. I could pass word to him that you want to arrange a contact with the acting leader. But I'd be very cautious. They aren't known for their hospitality. The Red Thread Society operates mainly in the Chinatown around Belleville, the smaller of the two Chinatowns in Paris, in the 20th arrondissement. However, there is a rival triad that works in the other Chinatown, in les Olympiades, in the 13th arrondissement. They are more mysterious and haven't even named themselves, but the police call them the Ghost Triad. They are ghostlike."

Ren nodded his head. This all confirmed what Drew had found, but Ren thought the detective's perspective might add more details.

Detective Arnot continued, "We have arrested a couple of men we thought were involved with the Ghost Triad, but they refused to say a word. The gang has no identifying tattoos, piercings, or other distinguishing marks, so we're not even sure they are members. We don't have any connection to them, so you're on your own about them.

"They're unlike the Red Thread Society, which has readily identifiable tattoos. It's almost like the Ghost Triad keeps to the admonishment of the Old Testament forbidding the 'marking' of the body, but most likely this absence is their effort to maintain secrecy. The Red Thread members, by comparison, seem to want to be identified. Their members always have a coiled red string or thread surrounding a two-headed eagle tattooed on their body, usually the left upper arm.

"The two-headed eagle as a symbol has been in use since about 4000 BC—with the Hittites, as a symbol for their sun god, and the Sumerians, as the god of their city. Now it is more usually associated with the Holy Roman Empire, the House of Habsburg, and the Romanovs of Russia. It was even used by England in the mid-sixteenth century. It currently is used by over twenty-eight countries on their flag, currency, or seals. Here it represents the triad looking east to their homeland and the resplendent glory of its past while also looking west for the future and its opportunity. The coiled string, the red thread, derives from an old Chinese proverb that goes something like, "An invisible red thread connects those who are destined to meet regardless of time or circumstance. The thread may tangle or stretch but will never break." The red thread seems to unite all of that triad into a close family unit. It's almost impossible to have an informant on the inside. We are fortunate to have one, even if he is only on the edge of the society."

"How do you know so much about this?" Ren asked. "I'm impressed."

"I was assigned to the gang task force for a couple of years. We had to study the gangs, including the triads, and learn about their legends, beliefs, and traditions so we could better anticipate their responses to our policing. However, this hijacking is like nothing we've seen before. I'll have our contact try to get you a meeting, but I warn you again, these triads mean business. They are seriously dangerous. Get too close, and you may never be seen again."

"We truly appreciate your concern, but we have no evidence to go on and must look at any and all possible suspects we can identify," Ren said.

"If you find anything, please let me know," Detective Arnot said as he handed them another business card. "This one has my direct line and my personal mobile number."

As Alex and Ren made their way out of the police station, someone called, "Ren, is that you?"

Ren turned around and smiled. "Walter, I haven't seen you in years, not since the UN." Ren introduced Alex. "Walter helped me repatriate Nazi stolen art. He was there as the liaison officer for the French Consulate."

To Walter, Ren said, "It's great seeing you again. Are you working here?"

"I've been here for eight years now. I've worked my way up to captain. Ren, you look great. How are you, and what are you doing?"

"I'm doing well. I'm working out of Singapore."

Ren and Walter exchanged mobile numbers and pledged to try to see one another before Ren left France, or at least keep in touch in the future. Ren and Alex headed out to find a nearby restaurant for lunch. After a quick croque monsieur—a simple but luscious grilled Gruyère cheese and ham sandwich—and a half carafe of the bistro's house white wine, they arrived at the appointed time to meet with James and Thomas Pfyffer at Pfyffer and Sons Insurance.

In business since the 1800s, the company was located on Boulevard Haussmann in a building dating to the Haussmann period of architecture, when the beautiful boulevards of Paris were designed and constructed. It spoke to the Pfyffers' long family lineage in the insurance business in France and eventually across the world. Ren and Alex were ushered into a very impressive wood-paneled conference room just off the reception hall on the first floor. A large Venetian crystal chandelier lit the oversized room. Ren mused that when art first became the focus of Pfyffer and Sons' insurance business, the giants of the art world might have sat around this table.

Two well-dressed men entered the room. "Savile Row," Ren thought as the older-looking brother approached first. The younger brother followed, dressed entirely in casual Armani and looking very pleased with himself. Ren and Alex stood to meet the brothers.

"Sorry to keep you both waiting," the older of the two said as he offered his hand first to Alex and then to Ren. "Thomas Pfyffer," he added, introducing himself, and then, gesturing to the younger man, "my brother James." As they shook hands, Ren introduced himself and Alex, each handing the brothers their business cards.

"Please have a seat and make yourselves comfortable. I understand that your business is located in Singapore," said James as he took a seat next to Thomas. "In fact, we just recently closed our Singapore office. We both enjoyed our time in that part of the world when we traveled with our father as young lads and later as apprentices, learning the business at his knee, so to speak. But even with a corporate jet, it's difficult enough to get there, to make a physical presence worth our time."

"I know you're very busy, as are we." Thomas interrupted his brother's trip down memory lane. "How may we be of service?"

It was quickly clear to Ren that Thomas didn't waste his time on small talk, while James was likely a schmoozer who might just enjoy avoiding business. "When this appointment was made before we left Singapore," Ren responded, "it was explained that we've been engaged by the Martine family to investigate the theft of their possible Van Gogh. We understand that you've made good on the insurance payment of €10 million and so Pfyffer now legally owns the work, but it has not been recovered. We're here to do just that, to recover it and find the people who stole it."

"I repeat, how may we be of service, Mr. Merit?" said Thomas. "The police have already interviewed both of us and our employees and have verified all our alibis."

84

"How well do you know Peter Meir? Do you think he could have been involved?" asked Alex.

Ren watched James as Alex asked the question. James pulled a poker face and didn't respond. All of James's warm and fuzzy talk was gone, Ren noted.

"Peter is a complicated story, Mr. Merit," Thomas said with a touch of sadness.

"Ren. Please call us Alex and Ren."

"Peter was once a very important person to our company in his capacity as a well-respected and skilled art appraiser. But he was also important to our family and in particular to me. We once were close friends. Socially, we enjoyed each other's company. We'd spend weekends at his lovely family cottage, talking for hours at a time, sharing simple country meals we'd cook together. Art was his life until the day Peter agreed to help a dear friend he cared for deeply. His compassion cost him everything. There were no criminal charges brought against Peter, but he had at first denied an authentication and then recanted the denial on a piece of art, to help this friend purchase it at a lower price. The art world does not offer second chances. Peter was excommunicated from his world, and his life was never the same.

"We have not spoken since that time. I reached out to him, but I think his level of personal shame couldn't allow him to reach back. I think he believed that he had let me down professionally and, worse to him, personally. This new desperate Peter might have felt driven to something like this, but he never would have knowingly been part of hurting someone. Never. Believe me, this missing guard of ours lies heavy on my heart every night. He was sent to do this job by us. We bear responsibility."

Ren had to ask, "Mr. Pfyffer, James, is there anything you wish to add?"

"Well, Peter recommended our company to the family, so I blame him for getting us involved if he turns out to be responsible for this theft." He spoke in a cocky, snide, and superior manner. "And unless the Van Gogh is found, our company is out €10 million and we still don't have official assurances that the painting is authentic. Peter certainly has the knowledge and experience to make that call, but his authentication would just never be accepted. So, there we are."

Alex took the lead. "We both want to thank you for your time and frankness. We may need to talk further at a future date as our investigation proceeds." As she and Ren stood to take their leave, both brothers joined them.

"We'll make ourselves available anytime you need us. I wish you and your team success," Thomas said, shaking Alex's and Ren's hands before leaving the room. James simply nodded to them both as he followed his brother.

....

Ren and Alex headed to the Pompidou. They were so deep in their own thoughts that the ride through Paris was hardly noticed. The receptionist directed them to the office of the curator for the exhibition. Once they had been seated and had introduced themselves, Alex went right to the pointt of the things. "We're here to talk to you about the van hijacking several weeks ago."

"Yes, I've already spoken to Detective Arnot about everything," the curator said. "We here at the Pompidou knew nothing about the Van Gogh and were very distressed about the destruction of the art from Arles. We had to cancel that part of the exhibition, although we were able to carry on with the exhibition for other regions of France. The exhibition itself was a success. I honestly think the stories about the art destruction helped give it more publicity than it would have had otherwise and contributed to the success of the show. I'm sorry I can't be of more help. The police interviewed all of our staff involved in the exhibition. Their alibis for the time of the theft were all verified."

"Did anyone here know of the shipping schedule, or the route?" Ren asked.

"We knew within a couple of days when the shipment would arrive, but not the exact date or time. In fact, we didn't know who would be doing the transport until the day the shipment was going to be delivered. We got a phone call in the morning from Pfyffer and Sons that the art from Arles would be here that afternoon. That's all we knew. Late in the day, we received another phone call from them stating that the van had been stolen and the art destroyed. They told us the police were involved and we could probably expect a visit from them. No other information was given to us."

"Just to be sure of things," Ren asked, "you knew nothing about a newly discovered Van Gogh traveling in the same van as the art for your exhibition until the police visited and told you about it, correct?"

"That's right," she replied.

"If you think of anything, please contact Alex or me. Nothing is too small or unimportant for us to consider."

Ren and Alex stood and handed her their business cards. Alex said, "Thank you so very much for your cooperation." Ren opened the office door and they departed.

....

Ren and Alex had dinner at the Bistro Madeleine near the opera house, eating early to be sure to arrive back at the hotel in time for the evening conference call. The moules Provençal, mussels

87

steamed in a broth of butter and wine with a touch of garlic and a few other spices, was delicious. The mussels were complemented by a very dry Chablis. Ren soaked up the remainder of the broth in his bowl with his baguette. "This really hit the spot," he remarked. "This perks up my mood after such meager results so far. I just hope the request to meet with the Red Thread leader doesn't come back to bite us."

CONFERENCE CALL

Kat gave her report first. "We took the high speed TVG train from Paris this morning arriving in Arles in the early afternoon, we were so tired after twenty-four hours of travel, we just crashed and set our alarms in time for this call. So we haven't accomplished anything today, but we have an appointment with the director of the Art Institute of Arles tomorrow. We'll see what he has to say."

Harley added, "We lucked out. The entire Van Gogh Museum authentication board is in Amsterdam for a special meeting, which is why we're rushing to Amsterdam as soon as we finish here in Arles. Since they live in different countries in Europe, this saves us a lot of time and travel."

Ren spoke next. "Detective Arnot didn't have much to offer except to say that the blood they found at the scene matched Joseph Boucher, the guard. After investigating, they believe him to be a victim. He is still missing. As Arnot said, whether he's living or dead is unknown. The meeting with James and Thomas Pfyffer revealed a close relationship between Thomas and Peter until Peter's ethical lapse. James, on the other hand, suggested that he wouldn't be surprised if Peter turned out to be responsible for the theft that so far has cost their company €10 million. Thomas seems forthright, but James appears a little sleazy. I wouldn't trust him, but nothing concrete."

Alex added, "We also met with the curator at the Pompidou. No one there seems to have known a Van Gogh would be in the van. The police verified the alibis of those involved with the exhibition. So, nothing new there."

There was a pause as everyone digested all the information. "Drew, how'd you do today?" Ren asked.

"I did some deep diving on the backgrounds of all the potentials without finding much, except for some tenuous finances for Nixon, the Martines, and the secretary for the authentication board at the Amsterdam museum. I'll send an email of the complete dossiers to each of you when I hang up."

"Keep looking at Peter, Dean, and Pfyffer and Sons. They're our best bets at this point. Let's hope we find a promising path tomorrow. Good night, everyone—we'll talk again tomorrow evening, same time," Ren said as he ended the call.

As soon as the call ended, Alex returned to her room in their suite, and Ren picked up his mobile. He stood, just staring at the phone in his hand. He hadn't spoken to Shiloh since he had been with her in Singapore. He suddenly felt a bit reluctant. Would the magic they'd shared still be there if he heard her voice now? Ren wasn't accustomed to these feelings, but they sure were real. He pulled up Shiloh's number from his contact list, took a deep breath, and called.

"Ren," she answered quickly, sounding a little breathless. "I'm so glad you called."

He answered with a question: "Does it sound silly to say I feel nervous?"

A half hour later, Ren settled into bed. They had worked through their emotional reconnection, and he had caught up on Shiloh's progress in Prague. Ren had ended the call with a promise to try to steal a day together in Paris at the first opportunity.

As he turned off the light, for the first time in his life he missed the feel of a warm, fragrant body next to his … Shiloh's body. It felt somehow good to have this longing, this mix of pain and ecstasy. This was indeed a new world for him. How could it be that at his age, with all his life experiences, this was new? He had to smile with a touch of sadness at missing her. "This is indeed a new experience for me, a new world," he mused, and then whispered to the empty room, "Good night, Shiloh."

Chapter 6: DAY TWO

ARLES

The next morning, a short taxi ride delivered Kat and Harley to the art nouveau–style building housing the Art Institute of Arles. Its graceful, curving lines complemented a new addition that looked as though Frank Gehry had designed it. The curved archways and windows of the older part blended well with the metal-clad addition, making it difficult not to dawdle before entering. The old section seemed to say, "I'll be here for a long time yet to come," while the titanium-and-glass-covered curves of the newer section replied, "Yes, but I am ready to grow and look to the future." The interior was just as curvilinear. In the entry, a simplistically designed desk with a lone receptionist guarded a long hall that probably led to offices, studio spaces, and classrooms. She looked up as they approached and said in English, "How may I assist you?"

"I'm Harley Bechman and this is Kat Dubois. We have an appointment with the director, Monsieur Breton."

The receptionist punched in some numbers on her console and spoke rapidly into her headset. She looked back at Kat and Harley, gestured to an open office door on the left side of the hallway, and said, "You may go right in," still in English.

"I wonder how she knew to speak English to us," Kat said.

"We certainly don't look French, no berets," he joked.

"Harley, be serious. I'm always amazed that no matter where I go and how I dress, even before I speak, everyone assumes I'm American when I'm clearly Eurasian! I guess we just stand out somehow no matter our heritage."

As they entered the door, a short and somewhat plump man rose and greeted them. His balding pate and handlebar mustache reminded Kat of Hercule Poirot, Agatha Christie's detective hero. After the pleasantries were completed, Harley said, "We're investigating the art van theft on behalf of the prior owners of the missing Van Gogh, the Martines. We understand that it contained ten pieces of art your institute had accepted to represent Arles in a broad countrywide exhibition at the Pompidou. We'd like to ask you a few questions, if you don't mind."

Without waiting for a response, Kat slid to the front of her chair, asking, "What can you tell us about it?"

"Well," Monsieur Breton replied in excellent English, "I cannot tell you anything about the van theft, but I can tell you about the art and the artists. It was very exciting when the Pompidou called and asked us to supply them with ten pieces of art from different artists around Arles. They planned an exhibition showcasing emerging art in the provinces. It is such a shame that all this well-executed art was destroyed. The police asked if I knew that a presumptive Van Gogh was also in the van. I told them I was not aware of this. I certainly hope that it was not also destroyed. We at the institute had no knowledge of this Van Gogh before the police reported the theft and fire to us."

Kat asked, "Could you give us a list of the artists—all those who submitted, whether selected or not—and their contact information?"

"Yes, of course. Besides the students here at the institute, we spread the word and had about thirty entries. We selected ten to represent Arles. When I received your request for an appointment to discuss the robbery and fire, I surmised you would ask for such a list. So I had my secretary print one for you," Monsieur Breton said.

He handed the sheets of paper to Kat and Harley as Kat thanked him.

"Do you recall anyone who was rejected making threats or becoming so angry it concerned you?" quizzed Harley as he and Kat scanned the list of names.

"Not at the time, but after the art van and its paintings were destroyed, I recalled one artist who was extremely devastated by his rejection, Sean Belmont. His name and information are on the list I just gave you. He called the office and demanded to know why he was not selected. He felt strongly that this would have been his big break, and now he hoped the exhibition would be a dismal failure since he wasn't chosen. Originally Dutch, despite his name, he has been studying and painting in France for several years now. His art is very graphic, displaying blood, dismembered body parts, destruction from exploded bombs, and similar mayhem. He ranted about how we would not have had the courage to show the work of Goya, Picasso, Basquiat, and others who painted the real world of war and destruction. At the time, we discounted his ravings as the emotional outburst of the artistic spirit. Now I wonder."

"Are there any others?" Kat asked.

Monsieur Breton replied, "There were many disappointed, but none as emotional as Belmont."

Harley had a last question: "Did any of the artists know the transport date and route?"

"Each artist knew when his or her art should be delivered to the institute for packing, but not specifically when the pickup date was scheduled. I'm sure they could have guessed. Also, the employees in the conservation department and the storage and packing area would have known when to have the art packaged for shipping, but not the specific date or time of the van's departure for Paris, nor the route. I've made another list for you. I knew the pickup date and of course so did my secretary, but not the route. I told no one of this date besides my secretary, and I checked with my secretary and he denies telling anyone. And I must emphasize that none of us, including me, were aware that a potential undiscovered Van Gogh was to be aboard the same van. We and the entire staff involved have also spoken to the police and have been exonerated."

This last comment by Monsieur Breton signaled that the discussion was over. Kat and Harley rose and thanked the man for his help. They gave him their business cards in case he thought of anything else that might help them, and walked out of the ornate building.

"Where to?" asked Harley.

"Let's check out this Sean Belmont fellow first," Kat answered. They hailed a taxi and gave the driver his address. "It isn't far. Nothing is in Arles," said the taxi driver as he pulled away from the curb.

"Harley, I find it hard to believe that one artist would steal or destroy another artist's work. I think they have too much respect for the creative process, no matter how upset they might become at a rejection, to destroy art. If it was an artistic/political event in and of itself, then I might consider it. But this was not," Kat said.

Harley added, "Also, I don't think an artist would pay attention to all the details of this crime, including

94

stealing the tow truck, forcing an accident, gassing the van driver and guard, then burning both the van and the tow truck. If this were done in a fit of rage or jealousy, it wouldn't have been so meticulously planned. It doesn't make sense ... it's just too well planned."

By the time they finished their discussion, they were already at their destination. They exited the taxi and proceeded into the derelict-looking building in front of them. It was a three-story walk-up with graffiti-covered walls. The stairs were cluttered with empty wine bottles and old newspapers and smelled of ripe garbage. They knocked on the door of number 15.

The door was opened by a bleary-eyed man looking to be in his thirties with a scruffy beard and tousled scraggly hair down to his shoulders. "Looks like he had a bad night," mumbled Harley.

Kat mumbled back, "I think all his nights are bad."

When Sean Belmont had opened the door completely, he scratched out, in a raspy aggravated voice, "Who are you and what do you want?"

"I'm Kat and this is Harley, and we're investigating the hijacking of the van carrying art from the Art Institute of Arles to the Paris exhibition. I understand your art was rejected for the exhibit," said Kat. "Can we come in and ask you a few questions?"

Turning without a smile, he asserted, "I don't know anything!" and walked into his apartment. Kat and Harley followed. The smell of pot hung heavily in the air. "Yeah, I was upset and angry when they didn't select my work," Sean said. "They said it was too bloody, too horrific, too disgusting. Couldn't they see I was just following the artistic expression of many artists before me? I was bringing the idea of man's self-destruction into the twenty-first century, expressing the terrible horror of war, the effects of suicide bombs, IEDs, missile attacks. They didn't understand! They still

95

don't. Yeah, I was angry and made some threats, but I would never destroy another artist's work. This was my big chance to become a known artist, to succeed, to be recognized, and they kept it from me."

Kat, almost feeling sorry for the guy, asked, "Where were you at the time of the hijacking?"

"I was at a friend's house. He had been rejected too, and we were drinking and smoking weed to relieve the crushing disappointment. The cops already checked it out. I can give you his name if you want."

"That would be most helpful," said Kat, thinking that even if the police checked it out, it wouldn't hurt to confirm his story.

Sean wrote down the name and handed it brusquely to Harley. Harley's and Kat's eyes met—apparently Sean would rather deal with a man than a woman.

Harley and Kat rode back to the hotel in complete silence, each absorbed in their own thoughts. As they arrived, Kat asked, "What do you think?"

Harley answered quickly, "The police checked out his alibi, so it seems unlikely to have been him. Of course, he could have had some thugs do it, but I don't think he has the financial wherewithal to have pulled this off. He seemed sincere when he talked about not destroying art, but maybe that was a cover. I don't see how any of the artists could have known there was a potential Van Gogh in the same shipment. So I believe that rules out money or other interests as motives."

"I agree," said Kat. "I think he's a bit unhinged and down and out but not capable of something like this, just a bit whacko. Or maybe I should say he has an artistic temperament!"

They booked a two-hour direct flight to Amsterdam for midafternoon. While waiting, they made the many phone calls necessary to verify the alibis of Sean and all the other artists. As they finished, Harley said, "Both groups were sad. The rejected artists are unhappy because of their rejection, and those whose paintings were destroyed are unhappy for a different reason. Those accepted felt this was their chance to break out. Now the art is destroyed and the Arles portion of the exhibition was canceled. As Tolstoy said in Anna Karenina, "Happy families are all alike; every unhappy family is unhappy in its own way."

"Arles sure seems to be a dead end," Kat said. "Let's see if we have any better luck in Amsterdam."

AMSTERDAM

Kat and Harley arrived in late afternoon at the Schiphol Airport in Amsterdam. There were planes landing and departing every few minutes from around the world. Harley, who had been reading up on the airport during the plane ride, told Kat that many people thought the airport's name meant "ships' hell," in reference to the former lake upon which the airport was built. By the time they'd passed through passport control, their bags were waiting for them on the carousel.

The twenty-minute taxi ride to the Andaluze Hotel flew by as a talkative and friendly cab driver gave them a running commentary on the city. "Originally Amsterdam was a small fishing village built on swampy land in the thirteenth and fourteenth centuries. The canals were further developed and promoted in the sixteenth century, allowing tremendous population growth. Currently, Amsterdam has over 2.4 million people. And we have over 2,500 canal boats."

"Doesn't it get really cold in those boats during the winter?" asked Harley.

"Not really," he answered. "They are well insulated and have excellent heating provisions. Many provide a year-round living for their owners. As you've already seen, there are also many, many bicycles here. Over 50 percent of the city's residents use bicycles as their main transportation, which helps to keep motor traffic to a minimum."

"I'm impressed," said Kat. "I agree with Harley and think it would be cold and damp in the winter aboard a canal boat, and I think that bicycles would be a freezing way to get to work in the winter. Give me a nice car with heated seats anytime! I have another question for you. What are those large hooks protruding from the gables on so many buildings?"

"Many now are nonfunctional architectural adornments from times past. The city's houses were traditionally tall, narrow, and deep. That hook allowed for larger objects to be moved to the upper floors, as the stairs were steep and narrow," answered the driver. "The story is that long ago the taxes here were based on frontage, so the Dutch, being very money conscious, decided to make their homes narrow and tall. Sort of why the French developed the mansard roof covering the top floor, as taxes were based on the number of floors and those covered by the roof didn't count." Their guided tour ended as they pulled up to their hotel.

The Andaluze Hotel was ultrachic and very contemporary. As they entered, they saw a crazy quilt of contemporary art, with furniture that managed to appear both classic and yet somehow on the cutting edge. There was a wall of windows looking out over the Prinsengracht, one of the city's three main canals. Harley had selected the hotel for its convenient location, as it was not too far from the Van Gogh Museum. They had a meeting with the authentication board the next morning.

As they headed to their rooms, they agreed on a meeting time for an early dinner. Both of them were looking forward to the evening conference call with the whole team. They wanted to find out how their counterparts were doing.

PARIS

That morning, while Harley and Kat were at the Art Institute of Arles, Ren and Alex were heading to Peter Meier's apartment, hoping to find him at home. They didn't want to forewarn him with an appointment. His apartment was located in an old art deco building in the heart of Montmartre, the old artistic center on the Right Bank. Ren remembered past times spent in this 18th arrondissement around the Basilica of Sacré-Coeur when he was younger. After walking up two flights of stairs, Ren knocked on the door of Peter's apartment. They were in luck. Peter answered the door, dressed in casual chic but dated clothes. He invited them in as soon as Alex had explained the purpose of their business. The apartment looked sparse, and Ren noted with interest that there was nothing on the walls. There were several packing boxes, some still open and only partially filled with household items or books. There were also several wooden crates, which Ren and Alex assumed were holding artwork, scattered around the room.

"Can I offer you a coffee?" Peter asked, as if to distract them from taking a full measure of his apartment and its contents.

"Much appreciated," Alex answered as she took a seat on an aging but elegant chaise. "Black for both of us." Peter returned shortly, carrying three expressos on a small hand-painted serving tray.

Ren settled in an overstuffed armchair covered in silk damask as he asked, with a hidden agenda, "Are you moving in or out?"

Peter took a small sip of the hot brew. "I'll be moving soon. Not exactly sure where. My lease is up, you see."

"Unhappy here?"

"It's a great location. I can get anywhere in Paris quickly and easily, but I feel like a change. Maybe it'll change my fortune."

"Are you having difficulties?" inquired Ren, knowing full well the status of his financial health, courtesy of Drew's research.

"Not exactly, but it can always be better."

"I'd like to ask you about the hijacking and art theft," Alex asked as she returned her empty expresso cup to the serving tray. "Were you aware of the schedule or the route?"

"I knew it would stop in Paris and then go to Amsterdam, but not the exact timing or route. In case you plan to ask, I have an alibi for the time of the theft. The police have already checked it out and cleared me."

"Let me be blunt." Ren took a turn. "Why did you recommend Pfyffer and Sons to Dean Nixon and the Martines? Why didn't you give them a couple of names and let them choose?" Ren was unusually adamant in his questioning because of Max's theory of Pfyffer's involvement.

"I knew they had little money," he tried to explain.

"Hmmm," Ren said, thinking fast. Peter would have known that Max would agree to fund the expenses, since he had just verified the painting as a Van Gogh. The "little money" explanation therefore made little sense. Was there some collusion here?

Peter went on, "The art wasn't authenticated, so it would have been difficult to get insurance for anything even close to its true value. I knew Pfyffer and Sons would come the closest. The Martines also needed transport to Amsterdam. Pfyffer was the only company I knew that would insure and transport the art. Why do you ask? Do you think they're involved in the theft?"

"There's no evidence yet to support that, but since you recommended them, I wanted to ask your thoughts."

"Well, if you ask me, the two most likely culprits are the missing security guard and Dean Nixon. When he was taking me back to the airport, he said his real dream was to have a gallery in a major art city. I asked him if that didn't take a lot of capital. He agreed and said he'd have to save and find investors. Then he added, 'If I owned the Van Gogh, I'd have the money I need.' This made me suspicious about his being involved," said Peter. "Maybe he was sorry he'd told the Martines what he'd found in their attic, instead of just absconding with it. It also seems the security guard has just disappeared. Was he part of the scheme?"

"Did you mention this to the police?"

"No, they didn't ask, and I was advised at the onset by my lawyer not to volunteer anything, but only to answer direct questions. Safer that way. So I followed his advice."

Ren and Alex thanked Peter and left his apartment. As they walked out of the building, Ren remarked, "One way to deflect questions about your own involvement is to throw someone else under the bus. Maybe he's correct, though. Now I have some tough questions for Dean when we meet this afternoon."

. . . .

After Peter's interview, Ren and Alex grabbed a quick lunch on their way to interview Dean Nixon. They had arranged for an early-afternoon meeting, and the taxi ride was relatively short to the university area. Nearby were inexpensive student flats. They found his

101

building and entered. It was a five-story walk-up, with Dean living on the top floor. The building itself was shabby but clean.

"Why is it always on the top floor?" Alex asked between breaths as they climbed the steep stairs.

Ren reminded her, "Artists like light, and the top floor is the best place to get it, either with a skylight or a rooftop they could use."

"I know that, but he's not an artist. He's an art historian!" Alex complained.

After a subdued knock, Dean opened the door wide and asked them in. Before them was a prim and proper-looking young man who looked to be in his mid-twenties. They introduced themselves. He greeted them warmly.

"As you know, we've been asked by Max and the Martines to investigate the theft of the Van Gogh," Ren said.

They looked intensely at Dean. He appeared calm and collected. They noticed he was clean shaven and well dressed, though his clothing was showing signs of wear. Understandable. They knew his inheritance funds from his grandparents were running out, courtesy of Drew's background check. He offered them seats at a small table next to the couch, which probably doubled as his bed in this tiny studio apartment.

There was a scruffy paint-peeling wardrobe probably acting as a closet for his clothes, while the table served as a desk. Papers and other paraphernalia of a graduate student were on the floor in disarrayed piles. There were two small windows and a short flight of stairs leading to the roof. The walls were covered with a very outdated floral wallpaper that was peeling off in some areas. Covering most of the wallpaper were inexpensive posters announcing various art exhibits around France and one landscape painting that seemed out of place.

Curious, Kat asked, "Is it an oil?"

"No. It's a watercolor," Dean answered with no elaboration. "Can I get you anything? A glass of water, coke, or wine? The wine isn't too bad," he said kindly.

"No, thanks," Ren answered for both of them.

"As an art historian, you have only one painting on the walls. Why not more?" Alex asked.

"I can't afford original art. That one was painted for me by one of my artist friends," explained Dean. "That's the only original artwork here. But I just made an impulsive purchase for my mother's birthday. She loves Mary Cassatt's paintings, the famous American impressionist. I was recently in Montmartre and found a painting in a similar style, with the impressionists' tender pastel colors and soft brushstrokes. It was in a gallery named Contemporary Old Masters. They specialize in contemporary artists who paint in the older styles. It cost me €25,000, but I now have some money—more money than I've ever had in my life. It's from my share of the Martines' insurance claim with Pfyffer. My mother has been so kind and supportive all my life, and now I can finally give her a birthday present that she'll value forever. A big splurge, I know, but my mother deserves it. It's over there," he said as he pointed to a wrapped package leaning against the wall. "I'm flying out in two days to New York to give it to her in person."

"May we see it?" asked Alex. "I also love Cassatt's work."

"Sure," Dean said as he picked up the painting and unwrapped it. "I have to unwrap it anyway so I can roll it up and put it into that plastic tube," he said, pointing to a piece of PVC pipe leaning against his desk. "Makes it easier and safer to transport." He then placed the painting in Alex's hands.

Ren examined the painting as Alex held it. It was signed by the artist and was about the same size as the Van Gogh. He turned it over, and the back was covered with brown paper, not unusual. There was a sticker on the back with the gallery name and address. Ren committed the name of the gallery to memory.

Before they left, Ren asked, "Who do you think is responsible for this theft?"

"I honestly have no idea. One minute it was sitting in the Martines' living room, all crated and ready to go. The next thing I know, I'm getting a call from Pfyffer telling me it's been stolen. What I want to know is how could anyone organize such a crime so fast? It doesn't make sense to me," said Dean.

"I wish I knew. That's what we want to find out," responded Ren. "If you come up with any ideas, call me," he added, handing Dean a business card.

As they left, Alex said, "I hope your mother loves her gift. I know I would."

....

After leaving Dean's apartment, Ren and Alex were silent for a while. Then abruptly Alex asked, "Do you think there's a chance the Van Gogh is hidden underneath that painting?"

"I don't know, but it certainly is a possibility. It almost seems too easy. A long shot to be sure, but we can't take a chance if there's any possibility. He could fly right out of the country with it right under our noses," Ren replied, shaking his head. "If Dean did this, he's one cool customer, and we've certainly underestimated him from the beginning."

"I agree. The painting sitting in his apartment could be just what he said it is, or the Cassatt-style painting is just camouflage and he'll roll it up with the Van Gogh for transport. Or it's the Van Gogh and it's been overpainted with the Cassatt-style painting, using water-soluble paint, so it passes through customs without a problem."

Ren thought for a minute, then said, "We know he's leaving for New York the day after tomorrow. If indeed he has the Van Gogh, we can't let him take it out of the country. The complications would be enormous: dealing with different countries' jurisdictions, governments, and law enforcement agencies, not to mention Interpol, would tie up the resolution of the case for years.

"He'll have to pass through security at the airport. If he checks any baggage, we can have airport security go through it, looking for the Van Gogh. If he just does carry-on, as he said, he'll take the painting off the stretcher and roll it. We can have airport security do a 'random' intense search. They can separate him from his carry-on. This will allow a pat-down in one room, while in the other, agents can unroll the painting to see if it's the Van Gogh. If not, they can x-ray the painting to be sure it is not an overpainted Van Gogh. If all this fails, he can be released to continue onto his flight." Ren paused.

"What do you think?" he asked Alex.

"I see a couple of problems with it. How do we get the cooperation of airport security, and where does the x-ray unit come from, and how do we get him in the correct security lane to do all this?" asked Alex.

"We call on our friend Detective Arnot and my old colleague Walter. Walter's rank as captain and his connections should be enough to have airport security's cooperation. Also, I am sure Walter can arrange for the x-ray unit and technician. We need to keep Detective Arnot in the loop, as we promised. They can find out which airline he's using and the flight time, so they can narrow the time window fairly closely. That should help. They'll have the airline flag his name so when he checks in they'll see a notice and route him to a special security line where this 'random' search will take place. Does this make sense?" Ren asked.

"Yes, I think we have to try, even though the odds are slim. Are we going to be at the airport?"

"We don't need to be there, but I'd sure like to be there, just in case the Van Gogh is found."

Ren took out his mobile. "Let's see if Walter can spare us a little time right now." Getting a positive response from Walter, they changed direction and told the taxi driver to take them directly to the police station.

....

"Well, I didn't expect to see you so soon, Ren." Walter greeted them in his office and was joined shortly by Detective Arnot. Ren hoped Detective Arnot wouldn't be too upset that he'd gone over his head directly to his old friend. Detective Arnot's attitude seemed fine, and he even smiled broadly after Ren explained to them how they might find the Van Gogh and catch the criminal behind the theft.

"It's a long shot, but I don't think we can ignore the possibility," Walter said. "I think it's worth our time and effort. We certainly ran down a few false leads in our time at the UN, didn't we, Ren?"

"We sure did, but some of those long shots paid off," Ren agreed.

Turning to Detective Arnot, Walter said, "We need to make this happen quickly."

"Thank you both. Please keep us in the loop. We'd like to be there if at all possible," Ren said.

"We'll be in touch as things develop, old friend," Walter said as they all stood, the meeting over.

CONFERENCE CALL

Back at the hotel, at exactly 8:00 PM, Ren's mobile phone buzzed. "Hello, Drew," he answered and placed it on speaker so Alex could hear as the call came in from Amsterdam. Everyone was on the line. They all shared their progress of the day.

Kat gave her report first. "We interviewed the curator at the Art Institute of Arles who put together the Arles portion of the Pompidou exhibition. We received a list of all the artists who submitted work. We interviewed most by phone. We did personally visit one disgruntled artist. His alibi was solid. We're now in Amsterdam and will meet with the authentication board in the morning."

Alex went next. "We started our day at Peter Meier's apartment. He's packing up to move. We found that interesting; maybe he's fleeing the country? He explained why he referred the Martines to Pfyffer for insurance and transport, but not a convincing argument. He also told us he thought Dean and the missing guard were the prime suspects."

Ren added, "This was interesting because we went to Dean's apartment next and found out he was leaving for New York the day after tomorrow with a painting, a gift for his mother. We decided after leaving his apartment that there was an off chance this was a way to transport the Van Gogh out of the country. My old friend Walter Frazer from my UN days, is now a captain with the Paris police, and he and Detective Arnot have agreed to have Dean's luggage intercepted and inspected when he flies out. This may include x-raying the art if necessary."

Harley responded, "This sounds way too easy, but we can always hope."

"Exactly our thoughts, Harley, but we can't ignore the possibility," said Ren. "We'll know soon."

"Have a good sleep, everyone. Let's hope this will be the end of our hunt! But meanwhile we'll continue other possibilities as planned," said Ren as they ended the call.

Chapter 7: DAY THREE

AMSTERDAM

The Van Gogh Museum was located in the grassy Museumplein park, near the Rijksmuseum and the classical music venue Concertgebouw. This appointment time was perfect for Kat and Harley, as most of the authentication board members were departing Amsterdam for their various homes the next day. They only convened when they had an artwork to review for authentication. The receptionist took Kat and Harley into a simple but elegant conference room.

The board secretary, Maureen Jansen, welcomed them as they entered and asked them to help themselves to coffee and the pastries laid out on a side table. They both opted for black coffee. The large mahogany conference table, polished to a warm glow, was surrounded by comfortable modern desk chairs.

They were seated for only a few minutes, sipping their coffees, when the first person walked into the room. Harley introduced Kat and himself to the man, who replied in perfect English, "It is a pleasure to meet you. My name is Josef Haydn, and no, I am not related to the composer." He smiled, and the tension seem to lift from his shoulders. He was a frail seventyish-looking man whose suit hung loosely on his body.

"He seems tense," Kat noted to herself. Just as she finished this thought, an impeccably dressed man in perhaps his sixties entered the room. "He carries himself like royalty," she thought. In a deep baritone voice, he introduced himself as Lucas von Berger.

Just behind him, a tall, elegantly dressed woman, perhaps in well-cared-for fifties, walked in wearing a severely cut business suit, a stylish chignon hair style, and large diamond earrings.

Kat did the introductions this time. The woman's name was Victoria Schloss. "What a great name for this distinctive woman of obvious German extraction," Kat thought, knowing that Schloss meant "castle" in German. "She looks like she owns a castle."

Of course, Kat and Harley knew all their names, their alibis, their roles on the board, and their primary occupations, but they thought it wise to get the conversation going with a simple nonthreatening question. "What are your areas of expertise on the board?" Kat asked.

They took turns explaining each of their talents in brief terms. Josef Haydn was an expert on brushstrokes and had even written a monograph on the distinctive method of Van Gogh. Lucas Von Berger was more of a generalist on Van Gogh and secondarily worked at a prestigious international auction house. He was an overall expert on Van Gogh's life and works. Victoria Schloss had written many texts on the coloration used by Van Gogh, such as his tendency to select his colors to express how he felt about an object—more like an expressionist than a postimpressionist—rather than how the object really presented itself.

Josef took the lead and explained their process of authentication. "We receive more than 500 requests a year, but we only ask to see the actual work in about 1 percent of these cases. The final authentication approval decision must be unanimous. If a majority votes yes but it is not unanimous, we then pronounce the artwork as 'attributed to Van Gogh' rather than 'by Van Gogh.' Of course, the owners have the right to obtain other counsel, and if they make a reasonable claim and present us with additional documentation, then we would reconvene. However, the board has never been known to reverse itself. A rejection the second time would be a death knell for the piece and knock many zeros off the value. Almost all of the oil paintings we review are found to be by someone copying the style of Van Gogh, either as a student or as an attempt at forgery. I hope that's helpful to you."

Just then the door flung open with a crash. The last member of the board had finally arrived. A man in his thirties rushed in and took a seat. "Sorry I'm late, but I was involved in an important test I could not interrupt." He introduced himself as Christopher Smithson. "I'm an American here for a two-year loan from the Metropolitan Museum of Art in New York. I work there in the conservation and fraud investigation unit. I'm one of the world's leading experts on paint analysis."

Kat instantly disliked this brash American. In general, she admired Americans. However, he seemed so full of himself it was hard to appreciate his abilities. He particularly irritated her for some reason she couldn't immediately identify. Realizing he was still talking, she tuned back in.

"I'm a chemical engineer and have a PhD in chemistry and fine art. Paints have evolved over time. Their chemical content has changed. That's where I come in. I can take a miniscule amount of paint and analyze it. From the contents of the various colors, I can often give a defined time of when the painting was created. For example, white paint contained a lot of lead in the past, so-called flake white. In the twentieth century, lead was generally outlawed in paint, mostly because of its toxicity, but there is still some leaded

110

paint available in various forms for artists. But now mostly zinc white or titanium white is used. I can analyze white paint to see if it contains lead, zinc, or titanium. If a white paint contains zinc or titanium, I can place it after the mid-twentieth century. Further, in analyzing the paint of a proven artist's work, I can compare it to a newly attributed work to see if they are the same. This is not perfect, but it helps in trying to authenticate a painting," he announced with a grin. "I'm here working on a very new technique—touch DNA analysis of paintings—which may at last push the authentication process into the twenty-first century."

Harley said, "Ms. Dubois and I want to thank all of you for allowing us to come here today and for sharing your valuable time with us. We know how rarely these meetings occur. It is our profound wish to find the missing Van Gogh so that it may be delivered here safely for your authentication.

"May I ask if there is anyone in the room who might have any ideas not previously shared about how this theft could have occurred? We often find that an obscure or random thought can lead us to a solution we seek, no matter how unlikely it seems at the time."

He and Kat scanned the faces around the table as they shook their heads no, looking at each other to see if anyone would speak up. None did.

"Your work here is exclusively focused on Van Gogh," Kat said, scanning the faces around the table as she spoke. "Are any of you aware of collectors who covet Van Gogh's works no matter the source? And yes, I'm afraid that I am referring here to the black market. We often find such types involved in the disappearance of the art treasures we seek." They all sat in stony silence, suddenly looking very uncomfortable, as if being simply asked the question somehow tainted them with guilt by association. There was no response.

Harley tried another question. "Have any of you had any personal dealings with the insurance company that insured the stolen art, Pfyffer and Sons? We're also wondering what you may know about their reputation in the art world."

This time they got a response. Lucas said brusquely, "I've known the company for my entire career. They are a giant in the world of art insurance. They date back to the eighteenth century, for God's sake. I count Thomas Pfyffer as a friend and an esteemed colleague. I'm certain that they are sorry to be involved in any way with this missing art. I find questioning their reputation repugnant."

"We appreciate your answer," Alex responded. "Every bit of information is important to us. Negative or positive, it all becomes part of our data to sift and analyze in our mission to find the missing art. We will leave each of you our cards in the event that you want to contact us. Any thoughts you may have—any opinions, no matter how disparate—could make a difference. And thank you once again for your time."

After leaving the board meeting, Harley made sure they were alone before asking Alex, "What do you think?"

Kat said, "I think the board members are clean. It's unlikely they were involved in any way. That is, except for the American, and also the secretary, though both have great alibis. The financials of those two give them a motive none of the others seem to have."

Harley nodded his head, agreeing with her assessment.

"I think a one-on-one with both would be good," Kat suggested. "Since it's about lunch time, why don't we split up and each take one to lunch? They might open up more easily over a meal."

"Sounds like a good plan. Food may ease the tension. Who do you want?" Harley asked.

Kat was very quick to answer. "I'll take Christopher Smithson. I don't like him for some reason I can't identify. Grilling him would be a pleasure. It'd be good for his ego. You can deal with Maureen Jansen."

"On it," said Harley, setting off down the corridor. He found Maureen's office back near the board room. The door was open, so he just walked in.

She looked up and asked, "How can I help you?"

"To be honest, I was hoping to have an opportunity to speak with you alone about the robbery. I also want to learn more about some of the procedures here at the museum. Would it be possible for you to join me for lunch today?"

"I'm not sure that I can help much, but I'd certainly enjoy lunch," she said. "Any reason to be out of the office. But I don't take my lunch for another fifteen minutes."

"That's okay. If you don't mind, I'll just sit here and review my notes. Just let me know when you're ready," Harley said.

Fifteen minutes later, Maureen picked up her purse and walked out the door with Harley. She suggested an outdoor food court nearby. It was a beautiful day with mild temperatures. She led them to a takeout stall with a sign in English proclaiming Good Food. As they walked over to place their order, Harley realized it was an American-style fast-food stall. They both chose the chili dog with sauerkraut and a Perrier. Finding an open table and chairs, they sat down to enjoy their lunch. Their drinks were still half full as Harley began some small talk, not his strong suit, to put her at ease. "Your English is perfect. Where did you study?"

"I've been speaking English since I was born. My mother is British. She met and fell in love with a Hollander while on vacation in Amsterdam. She never left. They both insisted that only English be spoken at

113

home so I would grow up proficient, realizing it would be very important for me in the future. And it has been. It's one of the reasons I have this job. Dealing with multinationals requires a common language. We use English, the language of business throughout the world."

She looked demure with her tailored business suit and her hair cut in a simple pageboy.

"How long have you worked at the museum?" Harley enquired.

"About five years now," she answered, finishing her last bite of chili dog. "I love my job. The pay isn't great, but the work is fascinating. And I am surrounded by all this fabulous art. What more could I ask?"

"It sounds ideal. Tell me about your family. Are you married, have any children?" He knew the answers but wanted to see how honest and forthright she would be.

To his surprise, she answered, "I was married for ten years before we divorced. I have a son from that marriage, and he is nineteen now. Unfortunately, he has problems. He's a drug addict. Drugs are so easy to come by here. That's what led to the divorce. My then husband wanted to abandon him. My son is now in a rehabilitation center on the outskirts of Amsterdam. It's excellent and has a very successful track record, but it's very expensive, which stretches my funds. What else can I do? He's my son."

"It must be very difficult for you," Harley responded.

"I manage" was her reply. They continued with small talk until Harley thought she was comfortable enough with him to begin the questioning.

"How involved with the authentication process are you?" Harley began.

"Well, I don't do any of the verifying. I just take notes and write letters explaining the process to clients," she answered.

"Does the museum arrange the shipping of art?"

"No, the owners take care of that. Very few artworks are actually reviewed firsthand by the board. Those requested are shipped and insured by the owners of the work. But we must know the schedule to arrange the experts' availability. I make arrangements for the artwork's intake and security while it's here at the museum, and arrange the board meetings. Remember, board members are not on-site here at the museum but have other demanding occupations, some even in other countries."

"Do you know of Pfyffer and Sons, the insurance company for the missing painting?" Harley probed.

"Yes, certainly—they are very well known internationally. They are well regarded."

"So, you did know the expected delivery date and shipping method?" Harley asked.

"That's correct. Most artworks are air shipped, and I was surprised when I found out this piece was being shipped overland. That's about all I know."

Harley escorted Maureen back to the museum. He gave her his business card with his mobile number and asked her to call if she thought of anything, anything at all, and returned to the hotel.

….

Kat found Christopher Smithson in his lab.

"Hello, lovely lady. How can I help you?" he asked.

She rolled her eyes internally. Though Kat didn't particularly like this arrogant and brash man, she had to admit he was invitingly handsome. "I'd like to ask you a few questions. I was hoping that you might be able to join me for lunch so we could discuss the missing Van Gogh."

115

"I'd love to," he said with enthusiasm. "But first may I give you a quick tour of my domain?"

"That would be interesting," she replied, wondering what he could have left to share after his oration at the board meeting.

Christopher gave her the grand tour, explaining, again in too much detail, the function of each piece of equipment. He finished by pointing to a special x-ray machine. "If we take an x-ray, we can see if there is an older painting or a sort of first draft under the painting, sometimes a sketch, sometimes a whole artwork, either by the same artist or another artist who later reused an old, already painted canvas." He was telling her things she already knew, but she wanted to keep him talking. "Sometimes forgers will use an old painting from the era of the original so that when the painting is analyzed the canvas conforms to the same period, but the x-ray will catch that.

"But what I'm most excited about now, as I said at the meeting, are the advances with touch DNA—the ability to extract a small sample of DNA from a source such as a fingerprint and, with nanotechnology, extract and sequence the DNA. Here at the museum, we have many Van Gogh paintings and artifacts from which we have extracted small samples of DNA, and we believe, with almost 100 percent certainty, that we have now isolated the DNA of Vincent van Gogh. So to confirm an undiscovered Van Gogh, we can try to extract fingerprint DNA from the canvas or in the painting itself, and then compare it to the known sample of Van Gogh's DNA. It makes provenance infinitely more accurate, and it is next to impossible to fake. If this undiscovered Van Gogh had arrived, we could have used this technique to assist in determining its authenticity. This technology is a boon to the owner, allowing a sale to proceed more quickly with better assurance of an artwork's true author. I am so excited

116

about this. I believe it will make a great publication," he said with such passion that it was contagious.

"That's truly remarkable! Very exciting indeed!" she responded with real enthusiasm. She was thinking that this new concept could make a big difference to SALT's future work.

"Can we go to lunch now?" Christopher asked. "I'm starving!"

"I was about to make that same suggestion," answered Kat.

"I know a sweet little restaurant within walking distance. It's a combination of Japanese and Dutch. Does that sound okay?"

"It sounds strange but worth a try," Kat said.

As they walked along the street to the restaurant, Kat suddenly realized why she had so intensely disliked him on sight. He reminded her of Philip, her first love. "Oh my God, yes," she said to herself. "All those painful memories with Philip resurfaced, and I put them all on him." Christopher's appearance and his comfortable manner had raised long-lowered defensive walls.

"This is it!" Christopher's words brought her out of her head. He spoke with so much eagerness, it sounded as if he'd just won the lottery. Kat shook her head and smiled.

....

Kat opted for the maki sushi with hamachi, or yellow-tail tuna. Christopher ordered sashimi shrimp. "Do you know the difference between sushi and sashimi?" he asked Kat.

"I have a vague idea, but tell me from a chemical engineer's point of view." She certainly did know, but she wanted Christopher to keep talking. "As if I could stop him," she mused to herself.

"Sushi is rice flavored with soy sauce and vinegar, wrapped in a seaweed roll and then sliced. It's usually served with soy sauce, wasabi, hot Japanese mustard, and pickled ginger. Sashimi, on the other hand, is thinly sliced raw fish or seafood, often on a bed of sticky rice, placed in a special wooden box and pressed to make a perfectly rectangular portion that can be picked up by hand or chop sticks. Again, with the same condiments. How about a little cold sake with it?" Christopher asked. "It goes so well with the fish and rice. And besides, it isn't often I have the opportunity to have lunch with such an attractive and intelligent woman," he said with a big beautiful smile.

Kat ignored his comment and asked, "Why cold sake? I thought it was always served hot."

Christopher, in his element now, said, "Warm sake is fine, but it's often an inferior rice wine that's been warmed to hide its defects. It's like chilling a white wine so cold that you can't taste how bad it is. On the other hand, the best sake is served chilled. That way you can taste all the nuances of a finely crafted wine. It allows the distiller to show off his expertise. But that's enough about food and wine. Tell me about yourself. How did you end up being an art theft investigator? Seems like an odd job. You look and sound more like you should be working in an upscale fine art gallery."

"Interesting you should say that. I did initially work in a gallery in Hong Kong. My interest in art and my language skills seemed to fit perfectly. But many of the clients were not knowledgeable about art, and I found myself being more of a teacher than a purveyor of fine art. It was very discouraging. Then I met Ren Merit, the founder of SALT, and agreed to work for him on a contract basis, helping to recover stolen and lost art of all sorts. It is quite challenging and sometimes risky, but always rewarding. I travel, see great art, learn every day, and help recover invaluable art treasures. It's exciting, to say the least."

"Do you make much money?" asked Christopher.

"I beg your pardon. You're not subtle, are you?" Kat asked.

"No, I guess not. I've learned over the years that if you want an answer, it's best to ask a direct question and not beat around the bush," Christopher said in reply.

She wasn't about to divulge details of her financial health to this brash American. "I don't get a salary. I'm on contract, as are the other members of the team. After the expenses of a recovery, we share in the payout. If there is no recovery, expenses are covered by Ren and we get no money. We are all happy with this arrangement. We receive payment for our efforts and success, with nothing guaranteed."

Christopher smiled as he made his next comment. "If you thought my last question was brusque, you'll decidedly not going to like this one. Are you by any chance in a serious relationship at the moment?"

Taken completely aback by this so very personal question, Kat was speechless for a few seconds before she answered. "No, I'm not."

Changing the subject, Kat smiled and asked a question she already knew the answer to. "Do you have any siblings?"

"No, I'm an only child. My mother still lives in New Jersey, where I grew up. My father died when I was just finishing my undergraduate degree in chemical engineering. My mother wanted me to take a job at one of the big petrochemical companies that were eagerly hiring at the time. I wanted to continue to study for a master's degree in chemistry, then a PhD. I did eventually complete my PhD at Princeton. While I was there, I began to visit the many great art collections in the region, and unexpectedly I fell in love with art. I was especially interested in the science of

119

colors and paints, how they were made, how they changed when dry, and how they changed with time. And now with the advent of touch DNA, it is even more exciting. That's the main reason why I'm on loan to Amsterdam, though paint analysis also helped me obtain this position.

"I was extremely fortunate to find a job that combined all these interests, working in the conservation department of the wonderful Metropolitan Museum of Art in New York. A city full of art, from graffiti artists on the street to fabulous galleries to so many museums I couldn't count them all. My primary job there is to analyze microscopic pieces of paint taken from an artwork and, using new techniques, match the color so it can be used for in-painting. Unfortunately, I don't earn enough to live in New York City, pay off my debts, and help my mother. Maybe someday. That's why my two-year loan working here in Amsterdam is so great. I continue to get my salary, and the museum here covers my living expenses. That way I can save almost all of my salary to help pay down my debt and keep helping my mother."

At the end of his sashimi, Christopher said, "I hope you saved some room to sample some traditional Dutch sweets, such as oliebol and poffertjes."

"I don't know what those are, but I'm always open to sweets—my downfall."

"Oliebol are sweet dumplings with fruit inside, covered in powdered sugar. And if that isn't enough sugar for you, we should also share some poffertjes. They are usually street food, but here they are exquisite. They remind me of the beignets at Café du Monde in New Orleans. They are fluffy clouds of dough, deep fried in butter and dusted with powdered sugar."

"Sounds like the Dutch enjoy their sugar. Let's order some of both."

120

"Fine with me," he said as he motioned for the waiter and gave their orders.

Time was running out. Kat had to get to the heart of the matter. "You've been open about your financial status and have a strong alibi for the time of the hijacking, but you do need money. Why couldn't you have just sold the information about the painting and pocketed the money?"

"I guess I don't have an easy answer, but I'm sure the police have checked my financial accounts and you're welcome to see them. Wouldn't a sudden deposit of unexplained money to me have tipped off the police?"

"If you had it deposited to a secret account offshore, they could never trace it," Kat replied.

"You're right, I guess. I could've done that. But how am I supposed to have had contact with anyone wanting to steal the art in the first place?" he asked.

"You're computer literate. You could have found someone on the dark web, never revealing your name, and had the funds transferred to your offshore account."

"Well, Kat, I guess you just have to believe me," Christopher said.

Kat looked directly into his blue eyes and said, "For some reason I can't put my finger on, I do." After a few minutes of just staring into his eyes, she said, "Let me ask you another question, then. Do you know anyone at the museum who you think might have been involved?"

"I don't know the board members well, but they all seem dedicated to their job here at the museum. I doubt any would jeopardize their job, career, and reputation by committing such a crime. Too much to lose. Then there's Maureen Jansen, the secretary, who had all the knowledge about the art shipment. I know she couldn't have been directly involved, but she could have sold the information. She's very open about her

121

financial situation. But again, she would be putting her job at risk, and the possibility of going to jail and not being able to help her son would be a big disincentive to doing anything illegal."

"Yet desperate times call for desperate deeds," Kat said. "Someone was involved. We just have to figure out who."

There was a pause in their conversation, which was interrupted by the arrival of the desserts. When they came, Kat took the first bite of the poffertjes and smiled. "Indeed, they are lovely, and the taste is reminiscent of beignets."

"Exactly," he answered, a big smile on his boyishly handsome face.

. . . .

They walked back to the museum in silence. As they approached the museum, Christopher said, "I know you think I'm just another crazy American, but will you have dinner with me tomorrow night?"

Kat, not expecting such a question, paused for a few moments and just stared at Christopher. Her thoughts flitted from the ethics of having a social date with a presumed suspect to the physical attraction she was beginning to feel for him, and then she found herself wondering if maybe he would let something slip when he was at ease on a date. "Kat, how lame is that?" she silently admonished herself.

She finally gave him her answer. "Yes, but something simple, please."

"Wonderful. And I agree. My funds are limited, as you now know. How about a little bar near my apartment where I usually eat? It's like a second home to me. The owner, whom everyone calls Moeder, which is 'mother' in Dutch, loves to fill me up with her home cooking. She says I'm too skinny. My mother would love her."

122

"Perfect!" Kat answered, thinking that he had just won a bit of her heart.

"Super, it's a date. Can I pick you up at your hotel?"

She agreed that they'd meet in the Andulze hotel lobby at 9:00 the next night, as she explained she had to be in on a conference call at 8:00.

With a huge grin on his face, Christopher made his way into the museum as Kat continued on to the hotel.

PARIS

Ren and Alex returned to their hotel from an early lunch. When Ren opened the door to their two-bedroom suite, they were surprised to find that the maid seemed to have left the drapes drawn. The room was so dark, Ren had to feel for the switch by the door. When the light came on, it took a few seconds for their eyes to adjust.

"What the—" Ren began.

"Don't move and don't make a sound, or you're both dead," commanded one of the two Asian men standing on either side of them, guns pointed at their heads. He spoke in heavily accented English. They both froze instantly but ran Harley's survival training drills though their heads, trying above all to remain calm and keep constantly assessing the situation and their assailants.

The guns were too close to their heads to make any sort of defensive move, and these two looked mean enough to enjoy pulling the trigger. The man who had spoken held them in his sights while the other began a body search, and none too gently. Not satisfied with the initial search for weapons, the man frisked them again, this time apparently searching for mobile phones, which he removed, and any hidden wires, recording devices, or transmitters. Probably to his disappointment, he found only the mobiles.

Both men were dressed elegantly in handsome black suits, their slicked-back hair held tightly in knots at the napes of their necks. The man who had spoken earlier said, "We understand you want to speak to our boss. This is the only way to do it. Behave, and you will live." It was clear from his tone that he'd like nothing better than to kill them on the spot.

Ren, in a calm tone of voice, answered, "We understand, but who is your boss?" Guessing that they were looking at two members of the Red Thread Society, Ren and Alex realized that they were apparently about to get just what they'd asked for.

"You'll find out soon enough," the other man responded. "We're going to walk quietly out of the hotel—our guns will be pointed at you at all times. We can do it this way, peacefully, or we have other methods to complete this extraction, if you prefer. But let me assure you, you won't like them. Get moving and stay close."

They were prodded into the elevator, which was empty. "Thank God," Alex thought. "No chance some innocent will set them off or get hurt." They made their way across the lobby and out the front door, held by the doorman. He didn't like the looks of the four moving in lockstep but didn't interfere. A black SUV with tinted windows was waiting. Ren and Alex were placed in the back seat.

Just as Harley had trained them, both Ren and Alex tried to remember landmarks as they traveled through the city. Not as easy in reality as in training, they were finding. Eventually they were driven into an abandoned warehouse. Before they were removed from the car, their heads were covered with foul-smelling burlap sacks, their hands zip-tied. They were led, stumbling as they walked, to another vehicle, realizing as they did so that walking blind is a lot more difficult than it seems. Before they were put into a second vehicle, they heard splashing and smelled gasoline. Then suddenly there was a gigantic whoosh. They felt heat at their backs and the unmistakable roar of a fire. They assumed that the SUV had just been torched. It was probably stolen, and this way there would be no evidence left behind.

As the new vehicle started to move, Ren began to worry. "Detective Arnot warned us," he said to himself, "but I never anticipated this scenario. I shouldn't be surprised. We asked for this connection, the possibility of meeting with the acting head man while their number one was under arrest, and now we're getting our wish. Alex has to be scared too, especially after Kat's knifing during our last assignment. So far, she's remained calm—we both have. I hope we can keep it up and get something for the risk we're taking."

Under the smelly hood, Alex was trying to control her own demons by talking nonstop to herself: "I never imagined a hood causing such fear. It's enough in itself. I feel so totally out of control, claustrophobic. We talked about this with Harley, but again, the reality! I'm trying to calm myself, but I know there's no hope of escape or rescue from these people. We're totally on our own, and we asked for this. We could just disappear and never be heard from again . . . got to concentrate here.We're here to try to get information, we haven't done anything threatening. They'll find out what we wanted to see them for and then take us back the same way we came, hoods and all. We'll be okay. We'll be okay. Harley, I hope you're hearing this. I pray I can keep calm. It would help if I could just see you, Ren."

Many twists and turns later, and after a much longer ride than their first, they were taken from the vehicle—some sort of van, they both guessed later—

and shepherded into a building and up a flight of stairs. The unmistakable aroma of Chinese cooking penetrated the hoods. In the background was a din of rapid-fire Chinese. Usually the smell of Chinese food made Alex long to eat, but not this time. She could only taste the bile in her mouth. After a long walk through silent space, they were forced to sit on a hard surface. The hoods were at last removed, but their wrists remained bound by the zip ties. Some relief, at least.

Their eyes were suddenly blinded by a bright light shining from behind a figure seated at a desk. As their eyes adapted to the light, Ren tried to examine as much of the space as he could, but in reality, he could only see the area on each side of the figure in front of him. They were sitting in an elegantly furnished room, probably full of rare Chinese antiques. The walls were a soft muted gray, and the carpet a slightly darker charcoal. To the left of the man were two zelkova-wood Ming chests, with internally illuminated glass shelves. The shelves contained numerous small sculptures and other antiquities. On the wall to the right side was a similar cabinet, though this one held Shang bronzes.

The man eventually stood and walked around to lean against the front of his desk. His eyes now adjusted to the light, Ren saw that it was an ornate Ming dynasty desk of huanghuali wood. On top to one side was a large four-colored Tang horse, while on the other side was a double-screen computer.

"May I ask your name?" Ren asked as calmly and confidently as he dared, but in no way demanding.

The man, dressed in a long black tunic-like robe with billowing sleeves, responded in excellent English with only a slight accent. "I am the number two leader of our triad, behind our leader, Chou Bing. He will be home soon and take over his leadership role once again. In the meantime, I am honored to serve in his place."

Ren asked, in the same tone as before, "How do you imagine his release from jail coming about?"

The man responded, "He is wrongly accused. Our lawyers are at this moment collecting paid receipts for all of his art bought at fair market value from reputable galleries around the world. That will exonerate him. Unfortunately, the art was previously stolen and will be returned to its former owners. But no punishment will be set for Chou Bing. The weapons confiscated are a different problem, but our lawyers assure me that they will bargain for a hefty fine with no jail time for our members. So, Chou Bing will return soon."

Alex thought to herself that all those galleries were probably located in nations that did not have an extradition treaty with France or the EU.

"But that is not why you are here. You wish to know about our role in the art hijacking of a supposed Van Gogh. I realize you are aware of the fake tattoo caught on CCTV. Some on our council believe it was a setup by the Ghost Triad to cast suspicion on us in order to create turmoil and chaos in the hope of annexing some of our territory for their own use. Some even voiced a desire to go to war over this. Fortunately, I prevailed. No one wins in a triad war. Since then, I have been proved correct, as no move by the Ghost Triad has taken place."

"Why are you telling us all of this?" Ren asked.

"So that you can carry this message back to the police. You are being returned without harm as a message and messenger. We wish the perpetrators punished as much or more than you do. However, if you persist investigating us for any reason, the next time will not end well for you."

He pointed to two of the guards and nodded. Obviously this signal had been planned. The two guards pulled Alex and Ren up from their chairs and walked them out of the room and down a corridor. A door at the end opened into a large cavernous space. Probably a warehouse of some sort, but now empty. It was dimly lit. The leader had followed them. A large plastic tarp was spread on the floor in front of them, and a young man was immediately dragged in and forced to kneel on the tarp. Alex had to stifle a gasp at the sight of him. Ren was grateful for his training as a Marine. Neither wished to show their true reactions. The man's tattered clothes were stained with blood. He was naked from the chest up. Cigarette burns were visible on his arms and chest.

The leader said, "This is the man with the fake tattoo. Stefan is a Bulgarian who has admitted that he was involved in the art robbery and was paid extra to expose a tattoo on his arm for CCTV cameras in the area. However, he didn't want a permanent tattoo associated with the Red Thread Society, so he went to a henna tattoo parlor instead. He denies he murdered the van's guard, but he does admit that he helped dispose of the body at an accomplice's garage, Victor's Auto Works, in the 19th arrondissement. Stefan continues to deny any knowledge of who orchestrated this sham. He has just told us that he was hired and instructed in the hijacking by this Victor. Despite our extraction methods, he continues to deny us the opportunity to punish the originator of this infamy!"

He then walked over to Stefan and asked again, "My final question—who is behind this operation?"

Stefan just moaned and rasped out, "I swear on my mother's grave, I don't know."

The leader was handed a cocked gun by one of the guards.

"Please God, no don't do this. I've told you everything I know." He began to shake and weep as he begged for his life. It was of no consequence. His fate was sealed.

128

The leader walked slowly up to Stefan and placed the gun against the man's forehead. He said, "You are of no further use to me," and pulled the trigger with absolutely no emotion.

The sound boomed in the vacuous space. Alex almost passed out as she watched the blood and brain tissue ooze from the hole in Stefan's head. To herself she said, "At least his suffering is over."

As Ren tried to understand the mentality that held life so valueless, he thought how he now had the information he'd hoped for, but this man had paid for it with his life.

"Don't worry about this death," said the leader. "No body will ever be found. I assume you have what you came for now and will have no need in the future to investigate us. I will oblige you with twenty-four hours in which to interrogate this Victor for your own mission before we interrogate him in our mission to find the originator of this attempt to malign our society." He didn't require an answer and silently turned and left.

Ren's and Alex's hoods were immediately replaced, and they were once again driven off. After another ride that seem endless, their hoods were removed and they were not too gently ejected from the vehicle. Again, it took a few moments to adjust to the light, breathe in fresh air to get rid of the stench of the hoods, and feel stable on their feet. Spontaneously, they went into a reassuring hug. They just stood there in each other's embrace for several minutes before either of them could speak. They were both in a recovery zone.

Ren finally broke the silence. "Are you okay? Really okay?"

Without moving an inch, Alex answered, "I think I am. I think I just counted all my fingers and toes." She pulled her head back so she could look into Ren's face again. "You look mighty fine, mister. Oh, how I wanted

to see that ugly puss while I was under that hood."
They both smiled with a special warmth.

"Indeed. We need to talk about what just happened on so many levels, Alex. But first I think we should get off the street and get back to the hotel where we can have a few hours to relax, debrief, and recover."

"And take a shower. I don't think I've ever felt this dirty, even though I know this feeling won't wash off."

"Agreed, let's get out of here."

They'd recognized the street and knew they were a short walk to the hotel. When they entered the front door, the bellman greeted them profusely. "Am I ever glad to see you two. Are you okay? Those two guys you left with looked very scary. I was worried."

"Yeah, they had strange personalities for sure," Alex answered. "No, we're just fine, thanks for your concern." They headed up to their suite.

Two showers later, the two of them sat in fresh clothes, each with a whiskey in their hands. "To another SALT adventure," Alex offered as a toast with her glass. "We survived and now have valuable information!"

"Indeed, we do," Ren said as he returned the toast. "But it cost a young man his life. Not an innocent man but a human being nonetheless." Ren took a big gulp of the strong but smooth liquid. "I'm so sorry you had to see that, Alex. It wasn't something you signed on for when you joined SALT. You were amazing. You kept your cool when our lives depended on it ... we both did, thank God."

"We owe a toast and a big thank-you to Harley. His voice was in my head the whole time. All his training kept us alive today, at least it did me," Alex said.

"The same was happening to me too, Alex. That tough guy was right there with me every minute, barking orders one minute and talking me down to keep me calm the next. I really don't know what would have happened if either of us had lost it, but I'm certainly grateful that we didn't have to find out. The triad members have short emotional fuses, and as you saw, violence is second nature to them. Our lives meant nothing to them."

"To Harley!" they both said without a moment of hesitation as their glasses clinked and they swallowed the last of their whiskey.

"Feel ready to get back to work?" Ren asked as he took Alex's hand in his and gave it a squeeze, "Road warrior?"

"Let's do it! When are we going to track down this Victor? We only have twenty-four hours."

"I know," Ren said. "The clock is running on us, but I think we need to be at our best when we face this guy. I say we get the address for his shop; knowing which arrondissement will help. There can't be many Victor's Auto Works, and then we'll go first thing in the morning."

"Absolutely. My knees still feel like jelly, to tell the truth. I need a good night's sleep, and I'll be at my best. Watch out, Victor."

There was a knock on the door that gave them both a heart-stopping moment before a voice said, "Room service." Ren checked the peephole in the door before he opened it. The food they had ordered looked and smelled heavenly, and it was just good old hamburgers with crispy french fries. They ate ravenously. It was the best meal they'd had in a long time, they both agreed, truly grateful to be alive.

PRAGUE – SHILOH'S CHALLENGE

Shiloh had had to wait two days for her first meeting with Gustaf, so she had spent her time exploring the city. She discovered that the center of Prague was on UNESCO's World Heritage List. She and Jakup, her day-shift security man, explored Prague on foot. A native of the city, he was a perfect guide. She found this historic city an architectural wonder full of Gothic, Renaissance, and baroque buildings, both preserved and restored. The many churches with their singular and multiple spires gave the city its designation of the City of 100 Spires.

Milos, Shiloh's collector contact, met her in the lobby of her hotel the day of their appointment with Gustaf. Jakup drove them to Gustaf's art gallery. It was not far from her hotel, very near the famous Old Town Square.

Today all thoughts were on this meeting she'd anticipated for the last week. When they arrived at their destination, all three walked up to the gallery, but Jakup waited outside the glass-fronted building. He had given Shiloh a panic button to wear at all times. It would signal her security to come to her at once.

The sign over the gallery read Beru dan Beranda, with the translation Brush & Easel lettered under it. Inside, Milos and Shiloh, who was using the name Anna Peak, found a variety of art in many styles, from contemporary to some that looked like old masters. They were not kept waiting. The people working in the gallery knew exactly who was coming and why. A very large man—a bodyguard, Shiloh guessed—stepped out from behind a curtain and ushered her and Milos past the curtain, then through a set of double doors into a sumptuous room with overstuffed furniture. It was likely a viewing room for wealthy clients doing just the sort of deal she was there to conduct, buying stolen art from Gustaf's very private collection.

132

Gustaf was there waiting for them. "Gustaf, this is my associate Anna Peak. She's the curator for the collector in Asia. He has sent me a message confirming his wish to purchase the Lorrain we've spoken about, with no questions asked and Anna's silence and his as to its origin."

"Miss Peak, I assume that I may not know the name of this collector?"

"No, he insists on doing business anonymously. And in turn he has no need or wish to know your name."

Gustaf said, "Come back in three days at 10:00 AM and I'll have it here for you to examine."

"How can I be assured that you still have the Lorrain he wants? I don't want to wait three additional days and go home empty-handed. My collector would not be pleased with me," Anna said with the confidence of one who sees this small purchase as an annoyance, an unplanned stopover on her way back to Asia.

Gustaf, displeased with Anna's tone, eyed Milos but in the end signaled his assistant.

Within minutes he had pulled up the image on a laptop and brought it to Anna. She took it in her hands and looked at it carefully. "So this proves that at some point you did have this work, and I must trust that you still do have it in your possession?"

Milos began to sweat. "Anna, you accepted my word. I've seen it in his private collection. Why would I lie?"

"Because you're afraid of this man, perhaps?" She closed the laptop. "This is your delay, Gustaf. You might keep in mind that my client is a wealthy collector. This little piece is for a relative who has some sentimental attachment to it from the war. He wants this for her. It means nothing to him personally, except to make her happy in her old age. I assume that you may wish to continue working with us? Perhaps you possess true masterpieces in your collection that he might indeed covet."

Anna had hit his greed button, and he couldn't resist. "I can assure you the work will be here for your approval and purchase in three days' time. If it can be arranged sooner, I will contact Milos. Does that seem acceptable?"

"I will be here. I hope the painting is also. Milos, are we finished here?"

"Thank you very much, Gustaf. And thank you for your patience," said Milos nervously. He was not accustomed to having someone speak to Gustaf in such a tone. It clearly frightened him.

Gustaf's bodyguard escorted them back out to the front of the gallery and left them at the entrance. Jakub opened the door for them to exit.

Once in the car, Jakub told Shiloh, "I know that man, and I'm certain that he recognized me also as ex-army special forces. He knows that I'm not to be taken lightly. That's a good thing."

"Shiloh, you can't push Gustaf's buttons. He can be very dangerous. You'll fly away with the art, and I'm left with him," said Milos, wiping his face with his linen handkerchief.

"I had to let him know I am someone to be taken seriously, Milos. I don't intend to leave without this work."

Shiloh returned to the hotel and sent an update to Drew and then one to Rose to let them know that at last things were beginning to happen.

When she'd finished, she sat back in her chair, exhausted. The meeting had taken a lot of energy. She hadn't expected that. This was a new world for her, but she found it exhilarating.

Sitting by herself in her room, she thought of how wonderful it had been to hear Ren's voice the night before. She laughingly gave herself a hug, saying, "That'll have to do for now."

134

CONFERENCE CALL

At 8:00 PM on the dot, Kat and Harley, and Alex and Ren, were on their mobiles with Drew. Ren spoke first. "Well, Harley, Alex and I owe you a big debt of thanks. You saved both our lives today, and we don't think we're overstating that."

"Okay, I'll bite. Just what did I do today while I was in Arles and you were in Paris?"

Alex and Ren painted a vivid picture of their kidnapping and the murder they witnessed. How they wished it were a video conference call so they could see the faces of the other three in Singapore and Arles. But they could well imagine them. When they finished, there was stunned silence at first. They all were a bit numb.

Viscerally they had all felt each moment as Alex and Ren described it. They were a team, they were a family, and what happened to any one of them happened to them all.

This hit home. Kat actually felt a burning sensation in her just-healed wound from the stabbing a few weeks ago. And they all were reliving the gunfire and killing in the woods at the end of the car chase that had followed. Life had indeed changed for SALT.

"Well, I recommend a big pay raise for Harley," Kat piped up. "He's pulled us through again. I know I wouldn't be here either without his training. This business we're in, we play it for keeps, as we used to say as kids when it was all a game."

"You're right, Kat, it certainly isn't a game," Harley said in a somber tone. "And I know we all know it deep down, but today could have easily had a very different ending, for all of us."

"Are we all on board for what comes next?" asked Ren. "I never want to take any of you or your lives for granted."

"I'm ready, Ren," answered Alex, "starting tomorrow morning!"

The others in turn voiced their continuing commitment.

Drew, the voice from the wilderness, added, "You guys are all my heroes, you know. I'm back here at Central drilling down on data while you're all risking your lives. Yup! No other way to say it. You're my heroes. But just in case, Harley, I'd like to be added to your training sessions, if that's okay."

"Great idea, Drew, happy to have you."

"You know, Drew, I clearly missed that one. You should have been training with the rest of us all along. Yes, your work has been behind a computer, but we can't foresee when a piece of information might draw you into the field and put you in harm's way," said Ren. "We'll start as soon as we return, and I'll bet Harley may have some homework assignments from here."

"You bet. I'll send a reading list to you, Drew. Welcome aboard!"

"Wish you all could see the smile on my face!" Drew said. But they didn't need to; they all heard the enthusiasm in his voice.

"So, what we got out of our visit to the Red Thread Society today was the name and general location of Victor's Body Shop and the knowledge that Victor was the driver of the tow truck and the one who recruited and trained Stefan. Alex and I are going there first thing tomorrow morning to confront him. It'll be a case of 'talk to us, or talk to the Red Thread guys who will be coming next.' We're hoping that he'll be persuaded we're his best bet."

"So that's our tomorrow. What's happening in Amsterdam?" asked Alex.

136

Harley answered, "We had our big meeting with the board at the Van Gogh Museum. Sorry to say, we didn't pick up any leads for a connection to the heist from any of them. And Drew's background checks found that they were all clean too."

"Except for Christopher Smithson, the American on the board, and the board secretary, Maureen Jansen," added Kat.

Drew interjected, "Yes, I found that they both have financial issues that make them vulnerable."

"They both have solid alibis, but that doesn't rule out accomplice roles for either of them. So I took Maureen to lunch today to see what I could dig up," said Harley. "I didn't learn anything helpful, sorry to say."

"And I took Christopher," Kat added. "I got the grand tour of his lab before a sushi lunch, but no leads either from him. To be honest with everyone, this guy has struck a chord with me. One I haven't felt for a very long time. I know what Ren went through last time in Paris when he met Shiloh, and I don't want to keep anything from all of you, especially now. We're having a late dinner tomorrow, after our conference call, as a matter of fact."

"I'm glad you shared, Kat. Just be careful. It can be distracting, as we all know, and we all want you to be safe," Ren cautioned.

"I will. I promise, a promise I make to all of you."

"Well, before we wrap it up tonight, I had some luck today and discovered that Maureen and the guard at the museum had an affair. Guess where I found the info?" Drew quizzed rhetorically. "Surprise, surprise, not on a dark web search but social media. Be warned, as I'm certain you already are, don't ever post anything on these apps that you don't want the world to know and never forget. With emotions running high, people will say things on public media that they'd never say even to a priest!"

"Well, thank you, Drew," responded Harley. "I needed a fresh lead. I'll get back to both of them and see where it takes me. I also want to look into some other staff at the museum and will have some additional names for you to dig into soon."

"Send them through. I'm ready."

"I think that wraps it up for tonight," said Ren, sounding a bit weary. "I think we all need a good night's sleep tonight. I know that I do! There's a lot on our hearts and minds. I'm grateful that we're all here together tonight. Kat, let me know if I can help in any way. Good night, all!"

Chapter 8: DAY FOUR

PARIS

First thing next morning, Alex and Ren left for Victor's Auto Works in the 19th arrondissement. They stepped out of their cab to find a shabby-looking garage with two open bays on the front side. Several men were inside, working on the bodies of a car and a van. "Wonder if they're stolen and being stripped for parts, or if they're actually doing body repair," Ren said to Alex.

"Either way," mused Alex, "my money says this is a 'hot' shop where stolen cars are brought for quick cash."

"Well, let's get on with our game plan; the clock is ticking," Ren said as they walked to one of the open bays and asked for Victor. They were directed to the office in the back of the shop. "Office" was a very lose term. It was a crowded space piled with stacks of papers interspersed with bits and pieces of car parts. Inside was a middle-aged woman dressed in jeans, a denim shirt, and worn sneakers, her glasses perched on her head as she studied a computer screen. With his back to the door was a tall, skinny man with long greasy hair pulled back in a knot. He was dressed in a dark gray coverall stained with grease and dirt. He was talking on his cell, and a pencil rested over one ear. As they stepped into the small office, the woman turned and barked at them, "What do you two want?" At that, the man turned to look at them as he finished his conversation.

"I'll take care of it, Kate. Stick with what you're doing." Turning around to fully face Alex and Ren, he asked, "You two got a problem?"

"Well, yes and no. But you do, Victor. Can we talk in private?" His shirt actually had his name embroidered on it. Maybe this had been a legitimate business once, Ren realized as he answered with his name.

"Anything you want to say you can say in front of my wife. I'm a busy man," he answered dismissively, sinking into his chair.

"We can do it that way too," Alex answered. "We're here to talk to you about a hijacking about a month ago and a missing piece of art."

He suddenly swung his swivel chair around and stood up. "Let's step into the back," he said, gesturing with his thumb to a back door in the office.

After yesterday, Alex's and Ren's radar went up, and they went on internal alert. They were ready for anything. They followed him into an open work space in the back filled with auto-body parts and several expensive brands of cars that had been partially dismantled. They could see a large tow truck parked outside beyond three open garage doors.

"Are you guys cops? I have a right to know."

"No, and we're not interested in whatever sort of business you're conducting here," Alex answered as she gestured to the scene in the garage. "We've been privately hired to find the stolen art you took from a van, and we're interested in the other people who worked with you on the heist. We understand from Stefan that you hired him for the job and also trained him for it. Not one of your regulars, but a rookie."

140

"Stefan's a real loser. He'd tell anyone anything to save his own skin."

"Well, he told us about you and played out the whole scenario for the robbery," Ren responded. "He told us about the tattoo you ordered him to wear just for this job. Interesting choice, the Red Thread Society's mark. That may have been your downfall, Victor."

His face went white when he heard the name. "Not my idea—just part of the job."

He obviously knew that they had him, and he wasn't going to play cute and deny it. Ren thought that was a good start.

"Figured you didn't come up with a scheme to steal a €100 million painting," Ren told Victor.

Victor's eyes seemed to bulge out of his head, as if they might roll out onto the greasy floor if he suddenly coughed. He obviously had no idea; he probably never did on these jobs. "Yeah," said Alex, "that much!"

"Look, I get a burner phone in advance for every job and wait for the call with instructions. I never know who's on the other end, and I always destroy the phone after the job. Same with this one."

"But this time somebody went beyond the instructions, and the guard of the art van was killed. Murder moves a simple heist into a whole new world, Victor. It changed everything, didn't it?" asked Ren. "It was you or Stefan, and he says it wasn't him. I think it was you, Victor, and you've buried Joseph here in your yard. Yes, not that you'd care, but he did have a name."

They could see in Victor's eyes that he was feeling trapped. Alex piled it on, "And it gets worse, Victor. The Red Thread boss gave us twenty-four hours to get our answers from you, then they're coming to settle up. That clock is ticking, and there's no time to run. There's no place to run. If the Red Thread guys find you, all your wife will ever have are pieces of you,

141

if she's lucky. More likely, she'll just never see you again."

He was sweating now. It was running down his face, and there were large wet stains spreading under both arms. He actually was pacing now. "There is a way out for you, Victor," Ren offered, and Victor stopped on a dime and looked him in the face.

"Anything, anything but those psychopaths," Victor pleaded in desperation.

"Show us where you buried Joseph and turn yourself in to the police. There's a Detective Arnot who's waiting to talk to you. He's just a phone call away," Ren teased as he pulled out his phone for Victor to see. "It's him or the Red Thread—your call, Victor."

"I'll show you where the body is buried. It's out back, away from the garage. Stefan and I buried it together," Victor told them as he walked. "We never planned for anyone to get hurt, much less killed; that's not our business. He just woke up too soon from the gas and saw our faces, and we panicked. Stefan grabbed one of the gas canisters and hit him. He went down and he was dead. The SUV driver brought us back to the garage with the body, paid me extra to get rid of it, and drove off with the art. That's what I know." Victor stopped in a spot next to a small storage unit with a mound of freshly turned dirt. He got a shovel from the storage unit and began to quickly dig. The dirt was dry and light, and it didn't take him long to uncover a plastic tarp. There was clearly a body inside.

"We've seen enough, Victor," Ren said as he tapped in Detective Arnot's number on his mobile. "I'm calling Detective Arnot now; time is growing short."

"Is there anything else you think we should know, Victor?" Alex asked as the phone starting ringing. Victor hesitated, and Ren hit stop on his phone.

"I don't know if this will help me or not," he said, going back into the storage unit and coming out with a burner phone. "This is how they always communicated with me, and I found this in the well of the front seat of the SUV that drove us back here. I figured the driver likely dropped it at some point that morning. I thought with a dead body in the back and the job going bad, maybe it might help me someday. Here it is," he added, handing it to Alex. "You can give it to Detective Arnot."

"Wise choice, Victor. Maybe it will help us after all, but you hold on to it until Detective Arnot gets here—there may be some fingerprints on it."

Ren called Detective Arnot's mobile again and this time let it ring until he answered it.

"Will he get here before the Red Thread?" Victor asked with raw terror in his voice.

Ren checked his watch. "Yes, we've still got time."

"You weren't bluffing, were you?"

"No, we weren't, Victor," Alex answered with firsthand knowledge of Victor's alternative.

....

Detective Arnot arrived with lightning speed. Red-faced, he stormed through the garage to find Ren and Alex. Ren's report over the phone of Victor's confession clearly hadn't defused his anger. Just what Ren had expected, but he knew he'd done the right thing.

The detective's forensic team arrived right behind him and were already at work with the body. Victor had turned over the burner phone to him, with Ren's assurance that neither he nor Alex had touched it. Detective Arnot's number two had cuffed Victor and read him his rights.

Detective Arnot turned to Ren. "I don't know if I should thank you or run you out of my city."

143

"Well, Alex and I spent some time with the Red Thread acting chief yesterday, and that's how we got to Victor. He gave us exactly twenty-four hours before he was coming for Victor himself, and we gave Victor the choice of talking to us and turning himself in to you, or facing the Red Thread folks. It was an easy decision for him."

"So they picked you up, did they? Scary lot, aren't they?"

"You didn't exaggerate one iota. We know that we're lucky to be alive today, but we got this in exchange."

Detective Arnot just shook his head. "Go on and get out of here. I know where to find you when I need you."

Ren and Alex didn't wait for him to change his mind, and took off.

....

That afternoon at Charles de Gaulle Airport, Dean was standing in the security line for his flight to New York.

"This is taking forever," he thought. "I should have allowed more time." When it was finally his turn, he put his small duffle and the tube with his art on the conveyer belt. The scanner beeped as he stepped through.

"Sir, please step aside. We need to wand you; it will just take a minute." Finishing the wanding, the security officer asked, "Can I please see your boarding pass?"

Dean handed him his pass and the officer took a quick look. "You've been selected for a random detailed search. Please step into this privacy room. We'll take care of your things; they'll be examined separately."

"Did I do something wrong? I don't want to miss my flight."

"This was just your lucky day, I'm afraid. A computer makes the call. We'll make certain that you make your flight."

Ren and Alex were in a side room with Detective Arnot and two of his team. The x-ray equipment had been set up and the technician was ready. They'd been observing Dean from the minute he approached the security checkpoint. All was going according to the detective's plan. An officer brought Dean's duffle and the tube with the art into the room. The art was carefully removed from the tube with the gloved hands of the technician, who was well aware that she might be about to handle a multimillion-euro piece of art.

Everyone in the room hovered around her in anticipation. As she slowly unrolled the canvas, Ren and Alex saw the Cassatt-style painting Dean had shown them in his apartment. "Damn, no Van Gogh," exclaimed a disappointed Ren.

"Well, that's step one. Let's take a look underneath," ordered Detective Arnot, signaling the technician to continue.

She moved the small unit into position and placed a cassette on the table, then gently moved the painting and placed it on the cassette. "Would everyone please join me behind this shield," the technician said. "This will just take a second." The machine sprang to life, and it was over. "You can see the image on my screen. It appears to be a single painting, just the one we see."

"Merde, this would have been too easy," exclaimed Detective Arnot, frustrated. "It was farfetched from the beginning—nobody is that stupid, but criminals do stupid things. We couldn't take the chance he'd get it out of the country. This doesn't clear him, since he could still have it stashed somewhere."

145

"I'm disappointed too, detective," Alex said. "We all hoped we'd be celebrating right now. Thanks for all your efforts."

"I'll call Walter later and thank him personally," Ren said.

AMSTERDAM

First thing that morning, Kat and Harley headed for the Van Gogh Museum. They had decided that based on Drew's information the night before, the board's secretary needed another visit. Drew had discovered that Maureen Jansen had had an affair with a married security guard, but no name was divulged. They decided that Kat should take this one.

Kat arrived at Maureen's office without an appointment, wanting to catch her off guard. Since no one else was around, she went right for it.

"Hello, remember me?" she asked.

"You're one of the investigators on the missing Van Gogh. You were at the board meeting yesterday. How can I help you?" she asked.

Kat thought a straightforward approach was in order and said, "We have just learned about your affair with a married security guard a year or so ago."

She gasped, "What? How could you possibly know that?"

"You shouldn't have talked about it on social media. Using a false name helps, but it's not foolproof. It never goes away. It's always out there to come back on you. We were able to trace it to you even with a false screen name."

"Does anyone else here know?"

"I've spoken to no one about it, but in order to keep it that way, I need some answers. I need the guard's name," answered Kat.

After a long period of silence, Maureen said, "I beg you to say nothing about it. We could both lose our jobs over this and cause trouble with his marriage." She looked as if she was on the verge of tears.

"Looks to me like his marriage is already in trouble if he had an affair. I need to know who he is. And who broke it off and why."

Maureen hesitated a few seconds and then realized she had no choice. "His name is Jan Smit. He's worked here for about ten years. He works the evening shift and I often work late, so we got to know each other as he had to unlock the door and reset the alarm when I left. I was lonely. He was in a marriage he couldn't get out of easily. We shared time and talked with each other. It seemed to fill a hole in both our hearts. One thing led to another. We never really loved each other; it was just to fill a void. After a while we both admitted that we should just be friends, and so we mutually agreed to end the intimacy." She paused before continuing, "We still continue to talk and enjoy the friendship, but nothing more."

"No bad feelings?" asked Kat.

"No, the split was agreed to by both of us. We knew that we had risked our jobs and more."

Kat pressed on. "Did you ever mention the details of the Van Gogh's arrival?"

"I may have told him the date, but I honestly don't remember. I really don't know. I certainly told him how excited everyone was, especially with the documented provenance. I didn't know any details of the shipping except the expected arrival date and the fact that it was coming by truck. I needed the timing information so I could arrange a board meeting. Jan is an honest man and very trustworthy. He wouldn't be involved. Also, I know he was on duty at the museum when the hijacking occurred. You can review his time sheets and question the other guards on duty to confirm it."

"I will, and also question him. But I won't make any of this public unless I find something suspicious. You realize of course that he could have sold the information without being directly involved. Maybe on the dark web," Kat ended.

As Kat turned away to exit, Maureen said, "Thank you for keeping this secret." She let out a short sigh of relief.

"We'll see," Kat said, not wanting to let her completely off the hook.

....

With the information Kat had learned from Maureen, late that afternoon Harley went to interview Jan Smit. Harley went to reception and had the security guard paged to come to the front entrance. After a few minutes, Jan walked calmly up to Harley without any outward show of anxiety. His uniform was neatly pressed and he was ready to begin his night shift. He wore a large ring of keys on his utility belt, along with a black truncheon.

Harley introduced himself to Jan as someone working on the stolen Van Gogh case. He assumed that the guard had heard about it, perhaps from Maureen herself. "Can we speak somewhere privately?"

"Let's just step outside," Jan replied, pushing the exit door open for Harley and waiting for him to pass.

"We are looking at potential suspects who may have aided or abetted the people who stole the art. We look for motives. People who have need of money or have something to hide and are therefore vulnerable to blackmail for information about the timing and transport of the art, for example. Our investigations have uncovered some information about you and Ms. Jansen."

148

"What sort of information?" Jan asked.

"We know that you and Maureen had an affair."

Jan was speechless for a few seconds, obviously trying to control his emotions. "Yes, I admit it. But it's over now, that was some time ago."

"She told me she still confides in you as a friend," Harley said.

"That's true, we're just friends now. She has no one else to talk to about her troubles," he said.

"Just what troubles are those?" asked Harley.

"I'm sure you already know, but her son is in a very expensive rehab center. That has created a financial nightmare for her. She has had to take a second mortgage out on her house to continue the payments. But what else could she do? He's her only child!"

"Did she talk to you about the stolen Van Gogh on its way for authentication?" Harley continued to grill him.

"We talked about it; the entire staff talked about it. We were all excited about the prospect of an original oil painting by Van Gogh being discovered. The possibility had everyone talking. It was the event of the year, maybe the decade!" he said, becoming a little excited himself.

"Did she tell you when it was to be delivered?"

"As I recall, she only told me a day before it was expected, as she did the entire staff. We had to make preparations for receipt of the art, precautions against damage, and arrange security. It all happened very quickly. The day it was due to arrive, the director made a formal announcement at the staff meeting to be certain that all the details had been worked out and that everything was prepared."

Harley thought that sounded reasonable, but he had one last question for the security guard. "Do you have access to all of the offices, including the secretary's and the director's?" asked Harley.

149

"Yes, I need access, but I never enter unless there is a specific reason," Jan said defensively.

Harley decided that was not the last question after all. "So, you can look into their drawers, search their computers," he stated.

"I'd never do that. Besides, the drawers are always locked and all the computers have passwords I don't know," Jan said, now obviously angry.

Harley couldn't let go. "I'll bet the secretary has keys and knows the passwords. Maybe she shared that with you."

"I'm done talking to you. Never bother me again, or else." He pulled out his baton threateningly and walked off.

CONFERENCE CALL

Ren and Alex had a lot to share. They started with their visit to Victor's shop and the discovery of Joseph's body buried in the yard. "Victor's confession to Detective Arnot and his surrendering of a burner phone was facilitated by the threat of the Red Thread Society. Detective Arnot is having his forensics team check out the burner," Ren reported.

"That was quite a rewarding day after yesterday's kidnapping experience," said Harley.

"That's our good news," said Alex. "Our operation at the airport with Detective Arnot this afternoon didn't have such a good result. We examined Dean's art in security, but no Van Gogh! However, Dean's still not completely off the hook."

Ren gave Drew the names of Dean's friends and asked him to do some more digging. Harley asked him to please do the same with Jan Smit.

"Something's not right there. During my interview with him today he became too belligerent when I pressed him about his affair. I think there's something else going on."

"I didn't pick up any leads from Maureen Jansen. She came clean about the affair. I believe she was being honest with me," said Kat.

"I've made an executive decision, guys," Ren said. "I need a break for a day, and I think the rest of you here in Europe do too. We picked up this new assignment right on top of the last. We usually get a break with some time to get away by ourselves, but not this time. And now Alex and I just experienced a kidnaping, a murder, and finding a dead body all in less than twenty-four hours. We've been hard at it, and I'm hoping that a day off the case may give our brains time to unconsciously assimilate all of this and give us a path to the answer. Sound good to everybody?"

Alex replied, "Thanks, Ren. I know I really need to take a break, but I was reluctant to suggest it. Didn't want all of you to think that I was in a bad place about yesterday, but a little escape would really be a boost right now, even just a day."

"It's just what the doctor ordered, Ren," Harley replied. "As head of our safety training department, I should have been there ahead of you with this one. Sorry, but sure glad you got us there anyway."

"It's a go for me too, no jokes please," said Kat, "I'll spend the day with Christopher. You know, Ren, it's only an hour-and-a-half flight from Prague to Paris and not too late tonight to arrange a day with Shiloh for tomorrow."

"I won't ask how you just happened to know about the flight time, but I talked to Shiloh just before our call tonight and we're all set. She'll be here first thing in the morning. But thanks for having my back, Kat."

"Always!"

"Well, you enjoy your date with Christopher tonight, and everyone have a good day tomorrow. We'll talk tomorrow evening as planned," Ren said.

A FIRST DATE

Kat wished she had something really casual for this first date. A pair of slacks and a shirt, a jacket, and her flats were the best she could do. She longed for a worn pair of jeans, a T-shirt and fleece, and her favorite pair of sneakers. Kat was on time for her date when she arrived in the lobby, but Christopher was already waiting. He wore a plaid-shirt and khaki slacks.

As they walked together out of the hotel, he shyly touched the back of her hand with his, then smiled at her as he slowly moved his fingers around to take her hand in his. They both were acting like teenagers on their first date. They walked several blocks to Moeder's Bar. When Kat saw the sign, she had to laugh. "It's named for her, Christopher! You failed to mention that yesterday."

"Kind of sweet, don't you think?" he said, holding the door open for her to enter.

There was American music playing in the bar; she recognized Mariah Carey singing one of her favorite songs. It seemed to Kat that it was hard to escape American music in any bar around the world, but she thought this was a good choice.

Christopher steered her to a booth near the kitchen. "Welcome to my world. This is where you'll find me almost every night. I find it cheaper and more efficient to eat dinner here than find time to shop and cook for myself."

"It's hard to make it work when you live alone. We're lucky when we're at home base in Singapore— Maria and Alfredo spoil us with wonderful food, and we don't have to lift a finger. One of the perks of being part

152

of the SALT family. So, what are some of Moeder's favorites? Which I'd guess have become your favorites too."

"Well, how about starting with one of my very favorites: Bitterballen. It's a minced beef and vegetable stew thickened with a buttery roux, which then is chilled until firm and rolled into balls, breaded, and deep fried. I love to eat it with some of Moeder's homemade rounds of crusty whole wheat bread and slather it with sweet Dutch butter. And how about a cold bottle of Grolsch. And since I know you love sweets, how about Stroopwafel. It's two layers of baked dough with a caramel syrup filling. How does that sound?"

"Like my calories for a week, but it sounds wonderful! Do I get to meet Moeder too?"

"She's probably home. She starts very early in the day with her baking and prepping. She's got a wonderful cook who covers for her a lot at night. But I'm certain you'll get to meet her. She'll insist on it after tonight. Your appearance will not go unreported, I can guarantee." As he reached over to take her hand, a waiter came to take their order. "Hi, Christopher. The usual tonight?"

"Hi, Luuk. This is my friend Kat, and she'd like my usual with an order of Stroopwafel added."

"Hi, Luuk. Are you one of Moeder's sons, by any chance?"

"Yeah, just one of them. What we needed was sisters to help us in the kitchen." He laughed as he made the joke. "Don't tell Moeder I said that, or my wife—she's cooking your food tonight."

After Luuk left the table, Christopher asked, "Okay, how did you know he was a son and how did you know that he has brothers—three, as a matter of fact. Do you have some psychic skills you haven't shared with me?"

Laughingly she replied, "No, I just figured Moeder would need a lot of family hands to pull this off."

The evening flew by. Once the food arrived, they both ate as if they hadn't eaten all day. "Finger-licking good, Christopher. I love to eat with my fingers, and picking up these mounds of wonder and licking off the grease is sensational!"

After they'd ordered their second Grolsch, Kat thought it was now or never for her one question about the case. She'd warned him there'd be at least one tonight. "Have you thought about anyone else at the museum who might be involved in the theft?"

Christopher had been expecting it and felt relieved that he had an easy answer. Then he hoped they could get back to talking about something else. "No," he replied.

"Had to ask. It's my job."

"Understood. Is it too late for that dessert?"

"I'm ready!"

While they waited, Christopher asked, "I'm curious, how did you get involved with SALT?"

"Do you want the long version or the short version?" Kat asked.

"The long version. I know it's getting late, but I want to know all about you, Kat," he said, taking both her hands in his. Looking into her eyes, he thought, "There's something about this woman—I can't label it easily, but by God, I certainly feel it." The feeling was so strong, he wondered if he had said it out loud, but he knew that he hadn't.

At the same moment, Kat thought, "That simple action of feeling both my hands in his just took my breath away for a moment. It felt like a kiss, a tender kiss. Oh Ren, now I understand what you were saying to all of us about your first feelings for Shiloh just a few weeks ago in Paris!"

Reluctantly, Kat brought her head back to Christopher's question about SALT. "To get to the SALT question, I think that first you need to know about Ren Merit, the founder of SALT, my boss. We met at a gallery event in Hong Kong. There was a presentation that night on art and philosophy. It turned out that it was a topic that interested us both.

"Ren's first love is art, and while he realized early on that he does not have any artistic talent himself, he certainly appreciates the skill and talent of others. We have that in common. He's a very insightful and intuitive man who on the surface is quite logical and methodical. Both sides facilitate his investigative work. His logic drives his sense of morality and philosophy.

"After the presentation, we were both assigned to be on a panel about spirituality in art. I promoted the idea that in times past, spirituality was equated with religiosity. That meant that spirituality in art was depicted as paintings of God, the Holy Family, saints, and religious scenes from the Bible until the Renaissance and then the Industrial Revolution. I took the position that spirituality and religiosity disappeared from most contemporary art.

"Ren disagreed. He took the position that there was only a shift in the definition of spirituality, that it was no longer tied to religion. In fact, he used Wassily Kandinsky as an example, pointing out that his art certainly is not paintings of saints or gods. Ren felt that Kandinsky's use of free forms and colors as abstractions was certainly spiritual, and he referred the audience to Kandinsky's book Concerning the Spiritual in Art. I had to agree, but I countered with the fact that modern art has lost that focus. I couldn't surrender the point. To this day, Ren feels that modern art is full of spirituality expressed by the depth, emotion, and passion he sees in works by Rothko and Pollock, completely separated from religion.

155

"A few months later, Ren was back in Hong Kong on business and we talked at length. I was between positions, and he had just completed renovating a colonial villa in Singapore for the headquarters of SALT, or Seekers After Lost Treasure. He had assembled a team with varied skill sets and backgrounds who were inquisitive by nature. He was searching for someone with a logical mind, which is a primary requirement for everyone, combined with intuitive talents, language skills, and a knowledge of art. He also longed for a second-in-command when he needed that support. I fit the bill on all counts, and he offered me the position on the spot.

"When not on assignment, we all live and work at Central, the name he gave to our headquarters. And here I am."

"I know, more than you wanted to know." The timing was perfect, as just then the desserts arrived. Kat smiled, as it smelled so delicious.

Christopher dipped his spoon into the caramel treat. "Not at all.

"Well, unlike this rich dessert, it could have come in smaller servings over time." Kat filled her mouth with a giant helping and moaned with delight. Christopher thought it was a beautiful sound.

"Ren surprised us all with a gift of time tomorrow," said Kat. "He's given us the day off, at least until our nightly 8:00 PM call to Drew in Singapore. Could you arrange a free day also? I'm sorry, would you like to join me? I should have asked that first."

"I can and I will! How would you feel about a day in Bruges? A day trip to Belgium?" he asked.

"I've only seen pictures, but it looks lovely. That would make it a real escape, out of the country!"

...

They talked about the arrangements as they walked back to her hotel, and he told her he'd pick her up to catch the train at 8:00 AM sharp. Once in the lobby, they spontaneously gave each other a big, warm hug. A hug they held on to, as if fearing it might be their last.

"Could we end this beautiful evening with a kiss?" Kat asked. The answer came not with words but with a soft, warm kiss. The best kiss she had ever had … ever!

"Well, that settles it," thought Christopher as he ended the kiss he never wanted to end, "this is my one." While hugging her a last good night, he murmured, "Kat, Kat, Kat. Where have you been?"

He continued in a regular voice, "Sleep well. I promise tomorrow will be a very special day." He turned and walked slowly away, pausing twice to turn and look at her until she finally stepped into the elevator. It took all his willpower not to run after her.

….

By the time she got to her room, her mobile was ringing and it was Christopher.

"I just checked the schedule, and if we want some decent time in Bruges we need to catch the 7:15 train. Can I pick you up at 7:00 instead of 8:00?"

"Absolutely, but this is my invitation, so I'll book the tickets online tonight. After all, you're throwing in guide service."

"Okay, see you bright and early. Sweet dreams, Kat."

"He has no idea how sweet," thought Kat.

157

Chapter 9: DAY FIVE

PARIS – ALEX

Alex had marveled at the Pompidou's brutalist architecture by Rogers and Piano, which she knew had not been appreciated by Parisians at large when it first opened. But the design's skeletal exterior spoke to her nuts-and-bolts esthetic. It was an inside-out building with all the functional apparatus—water pipes, electrical conduits, air handling tubes—on the outside of the building rather than hidden in the core of the building. She had to smile. "This is the sort of building I might have created had I gotten into architecture," she thought. The idea surprisingly pleased her.

"Okay, kid," she told herself, "Ren's not here, so do your own thing. How about sitting at a café and watching the world go by for a change? Idle the day away … no, you've never done that!"

Alex walked away from the Pompidou and all the tourists and turned down a couple of side streets. She found a small neighborhood café and took a seat at an outside table for two under the awning. There were a few workmen enjoying their lunch break, an elderly couple with a small furry dog at their feet, and a man who looked about her age sitting alone, studying the menu.

She heard the man order the plat du jour and decided to do the same, adding a glass of the house red. As she did this, the man offered a small smile of recognition. Alex took this as an opening, and never particularly shy, asked him, "Just what is the special today?"

He answered in excellent English with a hint of a French accent. "It's roast chicken, fingerling potatoes, fresh peas, and mixed greens—a real value in Paris for €15. Are you here on holiday?"

"No, just a down day from business, waiting for some research to come in. I'm not too good with down days. And you?"

"Much the same. I'm in from Geneva on business too. Waiting for a client to fly in for a meeting. I rarely have down days either, sort of at loose ends today."

"Well, I'm trying to push myself to make the most of it, for a change. My boss, more like our team leader, is a big art lover, and he had a whole day laid out for me as an art tutorial. But he is now otherwise engaged. There was one exhibition that really sounded intriguing, L'Atelier des Lumières. It's housed in an old iron factory known as Pichon in the 11th arrondissement. It's said to put the old sound-and-light shows to shame, using high tech to place the visitor inside the art rather than having them view it on a flat wall. Now it's featuring the works of two artists I really appreciate, Hundertwasser and Klimt. I'm heading there next if you'd care to join me on this rare-for-me cultural adventure?"

As the invitation hung in the air between them, the waitress arrived with their plates and wine. As she lifted each off her tray he responded warmly, "If you'll wait long enough for us to enjoy our lunch, I'll gladly join you."

The plates looked and smelled delicious. Just as Alex was about to take a sip of her wine, the man introduced himself. "My name is Hans, by the way."

Alex was glad she hadn't had a chance to take a drink of her wine before she heard the name Hans. Every bit of it would have left her mouth in an embarrassing spray. She'd thought instantly about the murderous villain by that name.

She must have gone white, because Hans reached over from his table and put his hand gently on her arm. "Are you okay? You're whiter than a sheet, as I believe the Americans say. Did I say something to upset you?"

Now she picked up her wine and took a long drink. "I'm sorry, but it's your name. It happens to be shared by a murderous German who almost cost the life of one of our team on an assignment we just completed for the Vatican. You don't by any chance happen to have a clever nickname?"

"Well, my ski mates call me Henri—pronounced without the H in the French style—because when I joined the group there was already a Hans. Will that do?"

"Henri it is, and by the way, my name is Alex." They both laughed, picked up their forks, and tucked into the simple and simply luscious plat du jour.

....

After lunch, they purchased their tickets and entered the Atelier des Lumières. They stood and looked around, as they were not only looking at a single projected painting but multiple paintings that changed and morphed into other paintings, bringing the spectators into the paintings themselves. The walls, ceiling, floor, and even special columns were covered with the paintings projected by the over 120 hidden projectors. Alex and Henri were engulfed by complementary music from over fifty Nexus speakers. It was total immersion. The illusion of being inside the paintings was complete. A completely different perspective.

Alex and Henri were both enthralled. "It's like nothing I've ever seen before," said Alex. "Ren will be so sorry he missed this."

"Well, I'm forever grateful that we met and that you introduced me to this truly magical, beautiful, and dynamic exhibition. I once saw something at a museum in Shanghai that reminds me vaguely of this but pales by comparison."

As they left the exhibition, Henri checked his watch. "Alex, this has been amazing. I can truly say I don't know when I've had such an entertaining, enlightening, and enjoyable afternoon, and it's all thanks to you. But sadly, I've got to go meet my client's plane." He reached into his pocket and pulled out a small case, then flipped it open and took out a white card. "Here's my information, Alex. If you ever feel in the mood to share another day like today, please call, text, or email me. I suspect that both of us are globe-trotters of sorts and might find ourselves not too far apart at any point in time. Does that sound like a plan?"

Alex took the card, read the information, and answered, "No promises, Mr. Churchill, and I won't even ask. I might just surprise you sometime in the future when you least expect it. Maybe in time to meet your grandchildren when we're both old and gray." They shared a brief warm hug, and then he put her into a cab and hailed the next one for himself.

PARIS – REN AND SHILOH

Ren met Shiloh's early-morning flight, and they headed immediately back to the hotel where Ren had arranged a lovely suite of their own for the day. Shiloh's first words to Ren had set their course for the day. "Ren, I need to be alone with you, now... please."

....

"Well, this is a wonderful way to spend a day in Paris." Ren had a big smile on his face as he delivered the room service lunch tray they'd ordered to the bed where Shiloh was arranging a pile of pillows against the brass headboard.

"I think it's perfect, and I'm starving." Shiloh snatched a hot croissant from the tray and tore it apart, popping half into her mouth without waiting to add butter or marmalade. She picked up the other half and offered it to Ren, who took it from her fingers with his teeth like a hungry lion and then grabbed a kiss in the middle of their chewing. They both laughed like little children who've just stolen a piece of birthday cake before the candles were blown out.

"If we're not careful, we're going to spill this tray, and that will be the end of our breakfast-lunch." Ren steadied the tray with one hand and pulled Shiloh closer for another kiss.

"Do you suppose anyone ever starved to death from too much lovemaking?" Shiloh asked playfully as she chose some strawberries from the plate, took a bit of one, and fed another to Ren.

"Not sure, but we could do some preliminary research," he answered with a devilish look in his eyes.

"Coffee first, pleeeeeze," Shiloh begged, "my only ask, and then I'm all yours."

Ren filled both their coffee cups and then downed a tall glass of ice water in one long swig, handing the other glass of water to Shiloh.

"Good call, I'm sure we're both dehydrated," she said, taking a drink, "and it's in my best interest to keep you hydrated." She picked up her fork and began to dig into her eggs Benedict Florentine. "Thank you for all this, Ren. If I weren't starving, I'd be weeping for joy in your arms right now. I'm just so very happy," she said, trying to get the words out as she gobbled mouthfuls of food.

Ren leaned over and playfully kissed the tip of her nose. "I know just how you feel, but we need some energy to get us through the rest of our day, so bon appétit." He carefully eased open the champagne cork and poured two glasses to wash down their brunch. "To the love of my life."

"And to mine." Shiloh tipped her glass to his and sipped the cold, luscious liquid, then kissed Ren, sharing the last bit across his lips.

AMSTERDAM – HARLEY

It was the first time in quite a while that Harley had had a day all to himself in a foreign city. When he first stepped out of his hotel, he felt a bit at loose ends without an assignment to track down a lead, search for someone, or follow a specific route. "Loosen up, enjoy the day," he ordered himself, realizing, not for the first time, that he worked better with orders, whether giving them or taking them.

Harley knew that he wasn't far from the Rijksmuseum, so he decided to stop and take another look at The Night Watch, one of his favorite paintings. The portrayal of men guarding, keeping watch, protecting the vulnerable and not so vulnerable, preparing to move out, seemed like the story of his life. As he stepped in front of the massive work, he was impressed by the refurbishment he'd read about. The new lighting had brought the painting to life again. The

163

last time he'd seen it, the room had been so dark that it was hard to appreciate the beauty of this masterpiece. Now he could see and feel the power of the work, the energy, the testosterone, emanating from Rembrandt's canvas.

A friendly museum guard informed him that they were about to start a very thorough layer-by-layer cleaning of the work itself and that it would eventually come to live in a plastic box—a very large box indeed—to protect it for future generations. Harley felt lucky to be enjoying it today with no barrier.

He thought of his visits to the Mona Lisa at the Louvre and Michelangelo's Pietà in the Vatican before the crush of humanity necessitated that they be placed behind protective glass barriers. It was the price of life, of progress, he thought. He had cheered along with his parents when the Berlin Wall came down, not really understanding at age eight, just what he was cheering about. He also remembered they had been crying. For them, it was a triumphant moment with heightened emotions. He had so much to learn, so much to come in his life. He gave a nod to the brave men in The Night Watch as if to say thank you and goodbye and left the museum.

Harley wandered for a while past the many flower stalls that trimmed the edges of the canals of Amsterdam: fresh cut, with their mix of fragrances, and potted plants ready to take home and be placed in flower boxes and small gardens. He had to keep reminding himself to be on the alert for bicycles. It seemed as though everyone in Amsterdam traveled on two wheels. In self-defense, he climbed into one of the boats that navigated the canals' quiet lanes of water meandering through the city.

Today the weather was beautiful, but he remembered well the shattering sounds that small pieces of ice had made on another hull as it pushed through partially frozen water one New Year's Day years ago. No number of insulating layers could keep a person warm on a day like that, and the cold floor of the boat under his feet had sucked the bone-numbing cold right up into his legs and beyond.

The boat eventually passed the infamous red-light district, and he enjoyed being a voyeur in passing, peering through the many glass window boxes that purposefully displayed the "merchandise." It was early in the day, so some were dark, but others were already occupied with scantily clad young women. The occupants ignored the passersby and appeared bored. Some were reading or texting, napping, or painting their toenails. Harley preferred his pleasures in privacy and in a time and manner of his choosing.

His stomach suddenly growled, letting him know it was time for lunch. He remembered having a hearty pea soup—Erwtensoep—here in the city and quickly found a small café whose menu offered it. He gobbled it up with a thickly cut slice of grainy bread that only seemed to whet his appetite. So he ordered Rookworst, a delightfully tasty smoked sausage. "How great this would taste with a Heineken," he said to himself as he enjoyed the first mouthful.

Harley polished off his day of freedom with a visit to a local AA meeting in English that he'd found online, and ended up having dinner with some of the locals he met there. It was one of the benefits of such an organization—a brotherhood, or sisterhood, of sorts. After an amazing meal at a restaurant he would never have found on his own, he made his way back to the hotel just in time for the evening conference call.

BRUGES – KAT AND CHRISTOPHER

Kat and Christopher made the early train to Bruges minutes before it departed. It was almost a three-hour trip to Belgium, direct but not nonstop. They went right to the dining car to enjoy their first breakfast together. The trip by train gave them the luxury of uninterrupted time to get to know each other. They hardly noticed the countryside as it passed by.

"Kat, you know my story, but I know nothing of your parents, where you were born."

"Okay, short version. I was born in Hong Kong. My parents still live there, working for a company that specializes in encryption. My father once worked with British intelligence and my mother was an early computer coder. I was schooled primarily in mathematics and cryptography, probably because of my gene pool. I speak Mandarin, Cantonese, Vietnamese, and—hopefully you agree—English."

"Ah, but you left out the part about inheriting your parents' good looks. You are breathtakingly beautiful, you know."

Kat just reached up and gently kissed Christopher on the mouth, then snuggled close to him, her head resting on his shoulder. The gentle sway of the train lulled them into a doze. It had been a short night for them both. They woke as the PA system announced they were pulling into Bruges.

....

Bruges had become Christopher's favorite weekend escape from Amsterdam. He'd rent a bicycle and spend his time exploring the city and, even better, the countryside, reaching farther afield with each visit. He'd gotten to know the hostels in the city and had found a few small farms that let rooms to tourists, all at bargain prices. But with Kat he'd focus on lovely Bruges, a wonderfully preserved and cared-for medieval city.

They strolled the old streets and admired the old architecture, even taking a small barge ride along the canal for better views and the purely romantic charm of the experience. Then they were off to the

166

Groeningemuseum, built on the site of the ancient Eekhout Abbey, to view the paintings of Jan van Eyck, Hieronymus Bosch, and Belgium's own René Magritte.

"What a treat to see Magritte's work in his home country. He's one of my favorite artists," Kat said.

"Something else we have in common. I really enjoy him too," said Christopher. "I love the mystery of his work. The details he leaves for the viewer to fill in. 'What's not there,' he seems to say to me."

"I know what you mean. And the way he loves to show disparate objects out of context."

Christopher finished her thought for her: "And exaggerates those objects both in size and scale, maximizing or minimizing them to jolt the viewer out of complacency. Yes!"

They both came to stand in front of Magritte's L' Attenant. Kat continued, "I don't understand it but I love his disparate juxtapositions. Why does he here juxtapose a rectangular column covered in sky and clouds rather than the expected memorial plaque, an apartment building seen through a large arch with a gigantic bell in front and a disproportionately large nude torso in a simple wooden frame? Other times, he depicts a self-portrait, but his face is almost never shown. He is turned away, or obscured by a bird, apple or other mechanisms to sort of say, 'I exist, yet I don't'".

"Kat, this reminds me of one of his other paintings. I can't remember the name at the moment. The sky and the upper treetops are in daylight, while a house in the lower half of the work sits in the dark with the house lights on. I agree with you, his juxtapositions are intriguing."

"You might say that you could create a whole philosophy from his work," Kat said with a sly smile, like the Cheshire Cat in Alice in Wonderland.

Christopher laughed and Kat pulled him close. "Watch out! I'll turn me into a philosophy geek," she replied, nuzzling him like a warm furry kitten.

167

They just stood there, not moving, until a noisy young group of children arrived in the room on a tour of the museum. They pointed and snickered at the couple as they passed them to exit.

Kat and Christopher left the museum and headed for a small café along one of the canals for two large orders of french fries with two glasses of Orval Trappist. As they began to munch on their french fries, dipping them in the mayonnaise, Christopher asked, "Did you know that french fries were actually invented in Belgium, not France?"

"I didn't know that, thanks for sharing. But I have to say I still prefer the American custom of ketchup for dipping. It's probably because I enjoy the sugar in ketchup. Which reminds me, we are going to do Belgian waffles with strawberries and cream next, right?"

"Already coming," said Christopher as the waitress arrived with their double order of waffles. "Shall we enjoy this with a coffee?"

....

They caught the 3:00 PM train back to Amsterdam to get Kat home in time for the nightly conference call. On the ride home, both began to turn their thoughts to the future. They had dinner together on the train, but neither of them had much of an appetite even after their light lunch. Finally, Christopher took her hands in his—although at that moment he wanted to take her into his arms more than anything in the world—and said, "Kat, I love you! I was going to say 'falling in love with you,' but the truth is I'm already there. Are you anywhere close?"

Kat sat still and quiet. "Yes, yes," she answered softly, feeling the tears welling in her eyes. "I hadn't put it into words yet, even in my mind. But yes, it's here in my heart. It's come so fast, and yet it feels so right. My

168

head is swimming, Christopher. It's a beautiful moment, but our lives are both so complicated. How does it work for us? How can it work?"

"We need time together, Kat, to get to really know each other. To make it real for both of us. To learn our personal quirks, our needs, the way we cope with the simple day-to-day issues of life."

"I don't know if we'd ever have a simple life together, Christopher. I'd want to stay with SALT even if I lived here, or in New York when you return. I'd work remotely, which I think could be a real possibility, but I'd be off on assignments for weeks at a time or for training in Singapore. Could you live with that?"

"I'd like to try, Kat. More than anything, I'd like to try. We're two very smart people—we'd make it work. We just have to decide to give ourselves the chance to find out."

They both sat with their thoughts as they picked at their food. When Christopher dropped Kat off at her hotel, they decided that they'd meet again after the evening call from Singapore.

"Kat, will you spend tonight with me at my apartment?"

"Yes," she answered, with a passionate kiss that said everything. "I'll call as soon as we finish."

CONFERENCE CALL

During the conference call that evening, Drew pulled a few rabbits out of his hat. He started off slow, then sped up. He was on a roll. "I found nothing else about the director or members of the authentication board. They all seem to be perfect citizens. Sometimes that's a warning, but this time I think it is true. The board secretary appears clean as well; nothing turned up. Her financial situation is precarious, as noted before, but nothing seems to have changed.

169

"However, I did find that Jan Smit, the security guard who was so defensive, was arrested as a juvenile. The court records are sealed, so I don't know the reason or the consequences. And another flag, his bank account received a €41,250 deposit three days after the hijacking. I am trying to track it down and have traced the wire transfer to the offices of a notary in Dijon. I'll speak with them when it's morning there. It certainly seems worth pursuing.

"The last item is about one of Dean Nixon's friends, Pierre Giacomo. Pierre shares an apartment with two other art students, François Gilot, and Rick Velarte located not far from Dean's apartment. It seems that Pierre works at a henna tattoo parlor in the Bastille area of Paris. Once that was a really rough neighborhood, but it has been gentrifying for years now. The henna parlor is flourishing due to the number of upwardly mobile young people wanting to sport a tattoo without having anything permanent that would be awkward in a business setting."

"Great work, Drew. Keep digging on that deposit to Jan's account and see if you can get a peek at his sealed court records," Ren said. "Anything on Pfyffer and Sons?"

"Unfortunately, nothing yet. Though I have some feelers out and I'm still checking into their finances and history," Drew answered.

"Keep at it. In the meantime, Alex and I will speak with Pierre Giacomo about the tattoo parlor as it relates to Stefan's tattoo. Kat, I want you and Harley to get back to Jan Smit about the sudden money deposit into his account. Go together. From what you reported, he could become violent, so be careful," Ren reminded them.

After a few minutes of quiet, Ren said what they all were thinking: "There's only one thing left in Amsterdam, the guard. Then we're at the end of our leads. The question now is do we start over, find another avenue to approach, or do we go back over the same ground to see if we missed other potential suspects or cleared a suspect we shouldn't have. Let's try to think of anything else. I most assuredly want to delve into the insurance company. I've sort of set them aside, as I wanted to clear up any peripheral possibilities first. But I want us to look at them with fresh eyes in the morning."

Ren added, "Let's all gather in Paris tomorrow and see if we can come up with any new ideas. This would be best done in person, so Kat and Harley, please fly to Paris tomorrow if reinterviewing the guard leads nowhere. If it gives you a fresh direction, call me. Alex and I will be here at the hotel."

"I'll book our flight right now," said Harley, "assuming we'll be able to take off as soon as we finish with Jan's surprise interview first thing in the morning. He's on night shift, so we'll catch him coming off duty."

"Sleep well, everybody. I look forward to being together tomorrow," Ren said. "Good night, Drew. Kat, will you stay on so we can have a minute?"

....

"Kat, are you okay? You know how distracted I became with Shiloh when we first met. Is it becoming serious with you and Christopher?"

"Yes. Now I so understand what you went through. I'm in love, Ren. For the first time in my life. It's all unfolded over just these few days, but everything's felt so right, like butter melting on hot toast. We've melted into each other's hearts, Ren. I can't believe I just used that metaphor, but that's exactly what has happened."

"You know that you'll always have a special place in my heart, Kat. Just be cautious. Let's talk tomorrow when we're together in Paris. Sleep well."

....

Kat let Harley know she was leaving for the night and would meet him in the morning at the Van Gogh Museum. She took a cab to Christopher's apartment. She had called on the way and told him about Paris. They both felt time slipping away. This was not how either of them would have chosen their first truly intimate time together, but they both felt the pressure of what if, for some inexplicable reason, this was both their first and last night together.

"I think I can read your mind, Kat, and I share your fears, but let's look at tonight as the first of many nights together for the rest of our lives."

They slowly undressed each other, touching each other's bodies as explorers, feeling the warm skin beneath their fingers. They climbed into bed and curled themselves tightly together, holding each other and wishing never to let go.

Chapter 10: DAY SIX

AMSTERDAM

Just as dawn broke, Christopher accompanied Kat out to a waiting cab and saw her off—along with his heart. As he walked back upstairs to his apartment, he thought how this was just the first of many partings they would have if they shared a life together. "Can we make it work?" he asked himself. "God, I hope so."

....

Kat and Harley met at the museum, as arranged, and waited outside for Jan Smit's shift to end.

"Let's be cautious," Harley said. "He has a truncheon but no other weapon I could see. Unfortunately, we have none. He'll be tired and maybe will let something slip. If he threatens us, we'll just back away. He was confrontational with me yesterday, and now, with our questioning him about the money in his account, he may become more so. I want to be sure we're prepared for anything."

"I agree on all counts," Kat said.

Jan suddenly appeared; it was time for him to unlock the museum doors for the day. He glared at them and said, "I told you I never wanted to see you again!"

"We need to talk, and if you don't agree, we'll go to the director and explain why," Harley said.

That seemed to take some steam out of him as he asked, "What?"

Kat, trying to diffuse the situation, asked, "Can we speak somewhere privately? We won't keep you long. I'm sure that you're anxious to get to breakfast; so are we." He was not happy, but he reluctantly ushered them into a small guard office near the entry.

"Jan, I'll get right to the point," Harley began. "We know about your time in juvenile detention. The records are sealed, but we think we can get around that, so why don't you just tell us what it was about?"

Jan looked daggers at them and said, "Once again, it's none of your business."

Kat didn't let go either. "Does the director know about this?"

Jan didn't respond, so Harley went for it: "We also know about the €41,250 deposit to your account from Dijon just a few days after the heist. Can you explain that?"

Jan began to fume. "That's none of your business either, and if you make trouble for me, I promise I can make trouble for both of you."

Harley didn't budge, and in fact stepped a little closer to Jan, crowding his personal space. "Is that a threat?"

"No. It's a promise," he said as he walked away from them without looking back.

Kat and Harley stood there dumbfounded for a few seconds before Kat spoke. "I don't like him, and he's very suspicious. Let's see what Drew comes up with tonight." She added, "Let's pick up our bags now and head for the airport."

....

175

Over breakfast at the airport, they talked about Jan and the euros. "The €41,250 deposit isn't enough as a share of the value of the art. And since he has an airtight alibi for the crime, maybe it was just a payoff for the information on the expected delivery date," said Harley.

"The wired amount would be enough for that," Kat said, her thoughts focused not on the moment but on Christopher. She needed to talk with Ren again.

PARIS

Ren and Alex headed out that morning to talk to Pierre Giacomo, Dean's artist friend. It was their lucky day. They found Pierre and his two apartment mates, François and Rick, huddled in their small apartment, looking over some artwork.

After they introduced themselves, Alex asked Pierre about the tattoo parlor.

"Yes, I work at a tattoo parlor to cover the expenses my graduate school scholarship doesn't," Pierre answered. "Is that important?"

"One of the hijackers had a tattoo that actually turned out to be henna," Alex said. "So, this is a connection for us."

"I can assure you that I had nothing to do with this robbery," Pierre responded earnestly.

"We may be starving students and artists," François broke in, "but none of us would do this. We worship the masters like Van Gogh. A new undiscovered work is truly exciting to us, but we just hope one day to see it, not to steal it."

"And none of us had any information about the shipping time or date that we could have shared or sold, much less arrange such a heist," Rick said with a passion Ren and Alex found convincing. "And Dean,

176

he's straitlaced, a straight arrow—he actually taught me that American slang. He'd never be involved with such a crime. He could have just bought the painting from the farmers for little money and not told them that it was a Van Gogh. They didn't even know they had it. It was the perfect opportunity, and he, like us, sure could have used the money."

"Excellent points, Rick, and an angle we've asked ourselves. We all have to wonder what we would have been tempted to do in a similar situation," Ren replied.

Alex added, "It seems hard to believe that any normal human being in that position wouldn't have been sorely tempted. Makes Dean seem like a saint, doesn't it?"

"Put like that, yes!" Pierre said with a big smile. "Can we get back to our studies?"

"You bet, thanks for your time," Ren said as they left the apartment. "Another dead end," he said to Alex. "We're due a break."

CONFERENCE CALL

Kat and Harley had arrived earlier that day from Amsterdam, and they joined Alex and Ren in their hotel suite for the conference call. Only Drew was on the other end of the line. After they discussed the non-helpful day, Drew dashed any hopes they had about a lead with Jan Smit. "I was able to sneak a peek at Jan's juvenile record. He was arrested for stealing a car and taking it for a joyride. He received no jail time, as he was only fourteen. He was told to stay away from his rather delinquent friends and complete three months of community service. The judge ordered the record sealed since he was a juvenile and appeared contrite, whether from being guilty or being caught was not mentioned.

"There's more bad news. I spoke with the notary in Dijon who initiated the wire transfer to Jan's account. He referred me to a lawyer, Monsieur Oiseau," Drew said. "Strange name, means 'bird' in French. I wondered what he looks like. Anyway, after I explained my interest, he readily agreed to talk about the wire transfer. He said it was no longer a confidential matter between lawyer and client since it had now been recorded in the pubic register for anyone to access. The wire transfer was for Jan's mother-in-law's estate. She died eight months ago, and her estate was recently settled. Her small shop was sold, and after outstanding debts were paid and the lawyer's commission was removed, the residual was €41,250. On the instructions of her daughter, who is Jan Smit's wife, it was sent to his account," Drew said.

Harley said, "That's too bad. I thought we finally had a possible lead."

"Looks as if Jan is innocent, or at least there is no evidence of his guilt," Kat added.

"One more thing before we end the call," Ren said. "Detective Arnot called today about the burner phone he got from Victor. He was able to trace the seller, but when he visited the tobacco shop where it was sold, the proprietor did not recognize a photo of Dean. It seems that Dean is off the hook as well. That leaves the Pfyffers, and maybe Peter."

"What if it was one of the other people involved?" Alex questioned. "Maybe you and I should pay a visit to the tobacco shop with some pictures tomorrow."

As they'd agreed earlier, after the conference call, Kat and Ren went down to the lobby bar and found a quiet corner in which to talk. Kat gave Ren a picture of the last few days of her personal life.

"I'm in love with him, Ren," she confirmed. "I can't believe that it has happened like this. So fast, so

178

unexpected. When I first met him at the board meeting, I thought him intolerable. How does that happen?"

"I know, dear friend. If it hadn't happened to me with Shiloh, I might find it hard to believe, but I know firsthand now. We're a long way from Hong Kong, aren't we? Neither of us was looking for this abrupt emotional change in our lives. Now we both have to deal with it. Max helped me take a leap of faith when I was on the brink and just not sure of what to do. I owe her for that. Maybe I can do the same for you now," he stated.

"I assume Christopher feels the same, right?" Ren asked.

Kat silently nodded yes.

"Then take a chance, Kat. Don't let this pass you by out of fear. It might not work out, but don't find yourself down the road living with regrets for what might have been. Sounds like an old cliché, but it's true, as Max reminded me."

"We're talking about my coming to live with him in Amsterdam when we finish this assignment, and working with SALT from there. Do you think that could work?"

"We can make anything work, Kat, if it's right for you." Ren thought a moment, then said, "As with Shiloh, this would be a life-altering change. Just as I took some time after we returned from Rome to Singapore, I'm pleading with you to let a little time pass also. For me it was just a couple of weeks and Shiloh was nearby, working on Rose's stolen painting, but I stayed away."

"I think you should come back to Singapore and take a breather. Then travel back to Amsterdam and see how it feels living together, if that's what you both still want. If it is, then it will be time to make a decision. I sincerely want you to be happy, but I want you to just take a moment."

With tears in her eyes, Kat responded, "Thank you, Ren. I know you love me, and I love you. Your experience with Shiloh has taught me many things. The most important is that when you find someone special, you don't let go. Your sense of logic tempered by love is just what I needed. I think you're right. I have to use my head and my heart to give us both some breathing room. Then if it still feels right, give Amsterdam a try and see where it leads. If it's the real thing, we won't lose anything by taking this time, except missing each other terribly." She moved closer to Ren and gave him a big hug.

Ren replied, "I think that everyone already knows you're in love with Christopher, but let's keep the possibility of your moving to Amsterdam private for the time being, so we can all focus on this assignment."

"Got it, boss!" she said, and gave him another hug.

PRAGUE – SHILOH'S CHALLENGE

To Shiloh, the days of waiting had dragged. Anxiety and loneliness took their toll. She could only eat so much kulajda, a delicious and hearty Czech mushroom-and-potato soup traditionally enjoyed with a small glass of Moravian wine. Jakup was even beginning to become a fan of the art district after touring it for days on end with an art curator.

As they approached the Brush & Easel to meet again with Gustaf, all Shiloh could think about was Ren. Her day with Ren in Paris was a gift, a magical gift. It was hard for her to believe it had been just yesterday. She longed for the holiday they had planned –the two of them alone on a warm, sandy beach in the Maldives, with time to really start getting to know each other.

"Okay, almost there." Adam had taken over on the security day shift. His words brought Shiloh back to the present. "After what Jakup told me about the last meeting's conversation. I'm going to be waiting inside the gallery today. I want to be closer to you."

Milos, who'd joined them at their hotel, responded, "I don't think that Gustaf's bodyguard is going to like that."

"It'll be fine, Milos. Relax, I have this in hand," Adam said confidently. "You have your panic button, Shiloh?"

"I have it right on my finger. Putting it in a ring was someone's ingenious idea. Thanks for checking, Adam; I'm all good. And remember, for this operation, I'm Anna."

The three of them entered the Brush & Easel together. Adam took up a position just inside the door. Shiloh and Milos walked to the back of the gallery, where they saw the bodyguard waiting for them.

"I see your friend decided to come inside today," noted the bodyguard as he led them back through the curtain and once again into the very private meeting room.

Gustaf greeted Shiloh like a friend—or a friend with dollar signs in his eyes, thought Shiloh. "Well, he got the message," she silently acknowledged.

"Anna, thank you for your patience. We're ready for you, just as I promised. I apologize for the delay." There was an easel in the center of the room with a drape over the piece of art resting on it. With a signal to his assistant, the cloth was pulled away in a dramatic flourish and the Claude Lorrain was revealed.

"There it is, Anna," said a delighted Milos. "Just as I told you. It's the very one your client is looking for, is it not?"

Shiloh knew immediately that it was indeed Rose's painting, but she stepped closer and examined it carefully as a curator. After a suitable pause, she

181

responded, "I agree. He will be pleased with the news." Stepping back and turning to Gustaf, she asked, "What is your price?"

Eager for this discussion, Gustaf answered without hesitation. "I think €1 million is a good price for your client. A similar painting by Lorrain was just auctioned in New York for $8 million."

"I think that you are a little high, Gustaf. But I must be in contact with my client before I can negotiate and we can complete the sale. This time it is I who must ask for a delay. I received a call on the drive here and was told that he has gone into a blackout period during the final stages of a large merger negotiation. I'm certain that you understand such things."

"Of course, of course. When will you be ready?"

"I've been told that by tomorrow afternoon I should be in contact. So we can complete the sale and wire transfer at that time. Assuming of course that we can come to an agreeable price."

"That will work, won't it, Gustaf?" Milos asked, not wanting to appear insignificant to the discussion.

Ignoring Milos, Gustaf answered Shiloh directly. "It will be my pleasure, Anna, and I have no doubt that we will come to a price that we both find agreeable. May this be just the first of many such discussions."

"We will see, Gustaf, we will see," answered Shiloh. "I believe we've finished here."

The guard stepped forward and escorted them back to the gallery entrance, where Adam was waiting. The guard nodded to Adam in recognition as he passed. The world of special forces in the Czech Republic was a small one.

....

As they pulled up to the hotel, Shiloh turned to Milos and said, "I don't think that you need to attend this last meeting, Milos."

"But it's the big moment, Shiloh, and I got you there."

"I know, and I thank you for that and you will be rewarded for your help. But this has to be me alone. Trust me on this. I'll call you as soon as it's done."

"I will await your call to report success then, but be careful, Shiloh. You understand with whom you are dealing. You are in my city, and I wouldn't want anything to happen to you," he said in a surprisingly fatherly tone and departed.

Shiloh went immediately up to her room and sent a message to Drew, letting him know that she had gotten the delay he'd asked for. She hadn't been given a reason, except Drew had said he was distracted with the Van Gogh case.

Next, she called Rose Stern to report. As expected, Rose responded, "A million euros! I don't ordinarily have that kind of money, but since the insurance company paid me its insured amount of €5 million, I could pay the million out of that. But if you recover the art, the insurance company will want all €5 million of their money back. I'd have to sell the Lorrain to have the entire amount I'd owe them, and that would defeat the whole purpose of your hard work. I don't know what to say."

Shiloh answered, "Let it be. I'll try to come up with another solution." Getting this painting back for Rose was a very personal matter for Ren, and it was her first chance to prove to him that she was a competent professional. She had to find an answer, and she wanted very much to find it on her own.

JULIETTE'S VAN GOGH

Chapter 11: THE MALAYSIAN TRAP

DESIGN

The next morning, Ren and Alex headed to the tobacco shop. They decided it was best if Alex waited outside and let Ren have a run at the shopkeeper on his own.

Ren, armed with photos of Dean, Peter, Gus the driver, the dead guard Joseph, and of course Victor, the operator of the tow truck during the hijacking, entered the tobacco shop and found the owner restocking his display case. "Hello," he said, extending his hand to the proprietor. "I'm Ren Merit and I'm working on a stolen art case. I know the police have already been here asking you to identify the purchaser of a burner phone, and you couldn't identify the photo they showed you. However, I'd appreciate you looking at these photos to see if you recognize any of these men."

The shop owner took the photos and looked at them very carefully. Suddenly he smiled. "Yes, this man. I remember him because he bought two phones. We sell quite a few phones here, but I've never sold two at the same time to the same person before. I remember him."

Ren thanked him profusely and left with a big grin. "Now we're getting somewhere," he said to Alex. "It's time to talk to Peter again."

Alex said, "Let's stop at the hotel and pick up one of those new Q-bug voice-activated micro listening devices that Harley brought. We can listen in on Peter after we leave, and maybe it'll give us a lead. We might hear a conversation with his cohorts if we've rattled him enough."

"Great idea." Ren smiled.

....

Ren and Alex went back to Peter's apartment and knocked. After a short delay, Peter appeared but only opened the door a crack.

"What do you want?" He was clearly angry to find them at his door again. "I told you all I know."

"Can we come in for just a minute?" Ren asked.

"No, I'm very busy right now," he said, trying to push the door closed. "Come back later."

Ren pushed back, opening the door wide, and brushed by Peter, followed by Alex. The flat was even more disheveled than before, with more boxes and crates, presumably containing artwork, scattered around the living room.

"I think you'll want to hear what we have to say." Ren pulled the photo of Peter from his pocket, holding it up for him to see. "The tobacco shop owner has identified you as the purchaser of two burner phones. The police have already found one of these phones in the possession of Victor, one of the people involved in the art theft and murder. This implicates you in the theft, and now that we know a murder was committed during the robbery, you are an accomplice to both crimes."

While Ren was talking, Alex managed to place the Q-bug in one of the open boxes. This would allow them to monitor any verbal communications from Peter's flat on Ren's mobile phone.

Alex now added for good measure, "And you should also know that Ren and I personally witnessed the Red Thread Society's execution of Stefan, the tattooed man who was in the tow truck with Victor. That's the biggest Chinese triad in Paris, in case you don't already know. We don't know yet if they've learned of your role in this. Also, the body of Joseph, the art van's guard, has been found buried in Victor's yard. Victor's now in police custody and spilling his guts."

"You're crazy," Peter said, though his eyes dilated and a small quaver entered his voice, "you're lying!"

"We'll be notifying the police that you've now been identified as an accomplice," Ren said as he and Alex turned to leave the flat. "I'm certain they'll be interested in talking to you again."

Ren looked over his shoulder and gave Peter one more chance. "Are you sure there's nothing you want to share with us before we leave, Peter?"

Peter stood his ground, speechless and wild eyed, and just barely shook his head no.

As soon as they left the flat, Ren turned on his mobile to monitor the transmitter. With a strong, clear signal, they immediately heard, "Hello, James, it's Peter. I just had a visit from SALT again. They know I bought the burner phones and are going to tell the police. They also said there are two murders involved. I denied everything, but I'm afraid." There was a pause. Then Peter spoke again, "Okay. I'll meet you with the crate at Le Bourget Airport at 10:00 AM the day after tomorrow. I hate waiting that long—I'd rather leave right now!" Another pause and then, "I know it takes time to make arrangements. I'll see you then, ready to go. I hope the police don't arrest me first."

....

When Ren and Alex arrived back at their hotel suite, Kat and Harley were waiting for them. "We have a real breakthrough and we need to move fast," Ren said to his team. "Alex and I just learned that Peter and his co-conspirator James Pfyffer plan to make a run for it and are flying out of Le Bourget Airport, with the Van Gogh, the day after tomorrow at 10:00 AM. We assume they'll use Pfyffer's company jet."

Harley immediately voiced the question that was on everyone's mind: "Are we going to notify Detective Arnot?"

Ren's rapid reply was "No—I've made an executive decision not to involve him at this point. We can't afford to be bogged down with red tape. We need to move fast. Better to ask for forgiveness than permission."

"Agreed. We need to catch them together with the art where there's no chance of escape. So timing is critical!" Harley said.

Kat added, "We need to set a trap. We need to entice them somewhere where they'll feel comfortable, and spring the trap."

"Just how do we do that?" asked Alex.

"Ah, it's time to call on Max." Ren reached for his mobile. "This could be her chance to carry out her revenge and maybe get to enjoy it firsthand. What we need is one of Max's fellow billionaires who wouldn't mind engaging in a little charade as a buyer for a stolen Van Gogh. Preferably one with an impressive mansion we could use. Is everybody drawing the same picture I am?" Ren got three big grins as an answer.

"We're getting there—I think all our juices are flowing after a long and frustrating dry spell," answered Harley. Kat and Alex spontaneously shot a thumbs-up.

It took a couple of calls, but Ren finally tracked down Max in Hong Kong and had her on the line.

"Progress to report, Ren?"

"Well, we think we'll have our two rats in a trap, with the Van Gogh, the day after tomorrow, but we need your help to set and bait the trap."

"And just who are our two rats?"

"James Pfyffer, as you suspected, and Peter Meier. Thomas Pfyffer appears clean."

"Wish you could see my face."

"Probably looks like ours right now."

"So how can I help with this trap? I'm all in!"

"They're flying out of Le Bourget the day after tomorrow at 10:00 AM. I haven't even shared this with the entire team yet—this is all happening very fast—but my next call is to Drew, to have him send an anonymous message to James offering to buy a Van Gogh for €50 million by wire transfer. His greed should draw him to the offer. What we need from you is a rich friend who has an impressive mansion we could use as the site for the deal and who would allow us to use his name in the email. Actually, somewhere near you would be perfect."

"Well, it's your lucky day, Ren. I have just the person and he's nearby in Ipoh, Malaysia. Let me reach out to him right now. He's just the man to go along with this. I'll call you right back."

"I've got Drew on my mobile," said Harley. "I filled him in while you were talking to Max. I think we caught all of your conversation—he's on speaker." Harley laid his mobile on the table with the team circled around.

"Hi, Drew," Ren said quickly, "we need you to join in fast, as you've heard. As soon as Max gets the go from her friend and we get a name, I need you to send an email to James Pfyffer from an anonymous address, offering to buy the Van Gogh. We'll settle on the wording after we hear from Max. Do you have a postimpressionist expert on your list of contacts that we could get to Malaysia fast?"

"I have a recently retired one in Hong Kong. I'm sending her a text as we speak."

"Max is calling," Ren said. "Hello, Max, what have you got?"

"Okay, our lucky day. Lee bin Osman took my call right away. He's all in, for whatever we need. I had no doubt he'd be up for it; it was just a question of catching this tech giant long enough to talk to him. We're old 'friends'—you're on speaker, aren't you?"

"The whole team is listening, even Drew in Singapore."

"Well, I'm an open book. So, Lee is a world-renowned art collector, with one of the largest and most prestigious collections of impressionist and postimpressionist art in Asia, and he is a certifiable billionaire. James should be convinced if he searches him on the web. Using his name in an email is a go, as is the use of a mansion he has in Ipoh, with a private landing strip. This should make James comfortable about landing. I'm forwarding you all the details now. He leads a tightly organized life and one of his chief assistants, a guy named Edward, with a click of his finger has sent me a file on the house with every detail you could ask for, including police contacts, names of key household staff, and his direct line in case we need something not covered. Now I have an ask, Ren: can I fly to Ipoh and be in on the takedown? I promise not to get in the way."

"We're in fact counting on it, Max."

"Thank you. I've waited a long time for this, Ren."

"I know you have, Max. I don't want you to miss this moment. Drew is coming down from Singapore and will pose as Michael, Lee bin Osman's right-hand man. Got that, Drew?"

"I'm already packed," he said. "I wish everyone could see the grin on my face right now!"

190

"Drew is also arranging for a retired Hong Kong art expert to be there to authenticate the art."

"If Drew knows the same person I know, it's Amy Fong. Before her retirement, she was the leading expert in this part of the world for postimpressionist art. Drew, if you need any help, call me. If she agrees, she can fly with me in my plane."

"You're right, Max. Amy Fong is the one we both know and the one we need," Drew said, pleased they both knew the same expert.

"Thought so. Drew, I'll connect with you and we'll work it out. This is going to be fun. Sounds like you'll be missing all the action, Ren," said Max.

"I'll orchestrate from here," said Ren. "This one has Drew's name on it. We just got your email file, Max, with all the information from Edward. We'll work out the details with him and arrange the setup in Ipoh so all the players have a clear plan. But first, that email has to reach James. If he doesn't go for it, it's all a no-go. We'll keep you informed, Max, and thank you!"

"Over and out! I'm here whenever you need me; just tell me what to do and when to arrive in Ipoh. Chou!" said a very excited Max.

"Drew has heard everything, and I've forwarded Edward's file to him," reported Harley. "And Kat and Alex have laid out a scenario for us to take a look at."

"Super, but first things first. We've got to send an encrypted email now; otherwise we don't have the bait out there. Drew, please jump in," Ren asked as he made notes on his computer.

"I've taken a crack at it and just sent it to you," Drew said. "Take a look now and give me some feedback and it will be done and off. Oh, and by the way, Malaysia doesn't have an extradition treaty with the EU."

"The lack of a treaty is a great piece of news, Drew," Alex responded as she typed notes on her laptop. "Kat and I can use that in the scenario we're developing for you in Ipoh,"

"Okay, Drew, I've got your draft up," said Ren. "I'll read it aloud so we can all have input—this has to sell James!"

```
Subject: Purchase of a
certain Van Gogh


    Mr. Pfyffer:


    I am an extremely wealthy and busy
    man in the tech sector who happens
    also to be an avid private
    collector of postimpressionist
    art. I live in a very large world
    of information and have been made
    aware that you may be in
    possession of a recently
    discovered Van Gogh masterpiece.
    To gain ownership of something so
    rare, something that no one will
    be able to view but me, fills me
    with excitement.


    I want the Van Gogh, and I want it
    now. And I am accustomed to
    getting what I want when I want
    it. If you deliver this work to me
    at my private residence outside
    Ipoh, Malaysia, within two days, I
    will wire €50 million to any
    account at your direction. You
    must deliver the work personally,
    and my art expert will be there to
    authenticate it while you wait.
```

Once the authentication is
complete, the money will be
transferred immediately, in your
presence.

Agree to this offer without delay,
and directions for your pilots and
yourself will be sent to you
within the hour. You will be met
at my private airstrip by a member
of my staff and brought to my
estate.

Do not delay with your response. I
am an impatient man.

Lee bin Osman

Drew added quickly, "The beauty of this is that if James takes the time to Google this guy, everything he reads will back this email up 100 percent. He's the real deal!"

"Comments please; the clock is ticking." Ren was clearly impatient.

Kat responded first. "Well, you made him sound like the perfect egoist, Drew, on target. Is he being at all too aggressive? We don't want to frighten James off, but we do want to push him, and this certainly puts the pressure on. This guy is all business."

"We know that he's getting ready to run, and this gives him a quick way out. He's got a protected place to land, a quick sale of the Van Gogh, and it all happens under our control. He's a greedy thief who knows his number is about up in Paris—he's desperate. I say hit send!" said Harley with great confidence in his voice.

Ren looked at the anxious faces around the table and saw no sign of disagreement. He said in a clear voice, "I assume you'll send a decryption key separately?"

"Yes, of course," answered Dean.

"Then hit send, Drew. Let's all pray we get a quick answer."

"It's gone," said Drew. "And good news: while you were reading the email, I got a positive response from Amy Fong. Her exact words are 'Thanks for bringing a bit of excitement into my rather dull retirement. Nice to know I'm still in the loop, so to speak, at least with you and Max. My go bag is ready (old habits die hard) and I await Max's takeoff information. Thanks, Drew, see you soon!'

"By the way, she copied Max on this too. So she's all set. I'm watching for James's email response like a hawk and awaiting my scenario for Malaysia. I've alerted Edward so he'll be ready to send the logistical info to James as soon as we get the nod. I'm leaving you on speaker so I won't miss anything there; you tell me when I can sign off."

"While we're sitting here sweating James's response, let's proceed with the scenario Kat and I have laid out with lightning speed." Alex scooted her computer over so both she and Kat could refer to the screen. "Someone needs to contact Lee's police friends and arrange their cooperation once we've outlined their role in our trap. Drew, can Edward help with that?"

"Consider it done. Just let me know when we get to that point." Drew added that task to the message he was typing now to Edward as he listened in on their conversation in Paris. Ren had always told him that he was the master multitasker, and he was certainly being tested today.

Kat began to paint the picture, starting with James landing at the private airstrip.

PRAGUE – SHILOH'S CHALLENGE

The moment was here. It was time for her final meeting with Gustaf. Shiloh had never felt so anxious and excited at the same time. Her adrenalin was pumping. She'd talked to Adam ahead of time and asked that both he and Jakup return to the gallery with her for this meeting and that one of them accompany her into the meeting room. Intimidation was very important to the success of her strategy.

When she appeared with two security men, the bodyguard was obviously not pleased, and he was even less pleased when Shiloh insisted that one of them stay with her when they entered the meeting room. But Shiloh was adamant and Gustaf was greedy, so he nodded to his guard to let them proceed and greeted the woman he knew as Anna.

Shiloh said to herself, "Step one accomplished." The Lorrain was on the easel, as before, ready for her purchase. "Gustaf, thank you once again for your patience. I spoke this morning with my client, and he told me that your price is too high."

Gustaf was obviously surprised, then disappointed. "What does he offer?"

Shiloh answered, "I think free is the right price." She said it with obvious emphasis on the "free." She wanted to be very clear.

"What do you mean?" Gustaf asked, flabbergasted.

"You and I both know that this work was stolen from a private collection. I'm prepared to call Interpol right now and expose you."

"So you want me to just give you the painting for your silence?"

"You can put it that way if you like. Your bodyguard knows my men and knows that we will walk out of this gallery with the Lorrain one way or the other. This painting, it turns out, is very personal to my client. It goes way beyond money. The Nazis took it once, you see, and my client vowed after this latest theft to retrieve it no matter the cost, but without any benefit to those involved with the theft in any way. It is a matter of honor, family honor. You just happened to get caught with it. This does not preclude any future dealings with my client. This is, as they say, a one-off."

Gustaf had no choice and he knew it. "You win this time, Anna. But I won't forget." He nodded to his assistant, who removed the canvas from the easel, placed it in the wrapping it had been transported in, and handed it to Adam. A red-faced Gustaf simply said in a low growl to Shiloh, "Go!" and walked out of the room, his bodyguard and assistant trailing behind.

As soon as Gustaf left the room, he told his bodyguard to follow Anna's car and took his mobile out and dialed. The call was picked up immediately. "Veronique, I've got a job for you and Sasha," he said, "and it's very personal."

Shiloh made sure the painting was securely wrapped, and then the three left the gallery for the last time. They drove immediately to the special art packing shop Drew had prearranged for her. They were waiting for her and quickly and professionally packaged the canvas for shipping.

....

Veronique and Sasha took over from Gustaf's bodyguard at the art packing shop. They continued the tail on Anna, looking for an opportunity to complete Gustaf's orders.

Shiloh and her guards took the small crate directly to the air shipper Drew had also arranged. "Drew's amazing," Shiloh said to herself as she dropped off the package with every confidence that it would be hanging in Rose's living room that night. This would be its last trip home to Austria, to Rose.

Shiloh and her security team returned together for the last time to the hotel. She had to pack and confirm her flight to Singapore that night. She had felt so confident of her success that she had also arranged for Adam and Jakup to join her for a celebratory dinner at the guards' favorite restaurant on the way to the airport.

But first she called Rose with the news. "Shiloh, however did you do it?" Rose responded. "I can't believe what I'm hearing. Will it really be home tonight?"

"It will, Rose. I'm so very happy it all worked out as you hoped. And there was no purchase necessary, so you can return the insurance money in full and treasure the painting for the rest of your life."

"That's a miracle, Shiloh. I will never forget you and what you've done for me. Please thank Ren and tell him that we'll be speaking very soon. Safe travels, Shiloh."

Shiloh knew that Drew was in the middle of something, so she didn't call but instead sent another text.

```
Hi Drew,

Just wanted to let you know,
mission accomplished and without
using any of SALT's funds. The
painting is on its way home to
Rose. I'm flying back to Singapore
tonight. See you soon and thank
you for all your help!
```

Shiloh

Lastly, Shiloh thought she owed Milos a heads-up. She knew that she had put him in potential danger.

"What have you done?" Milos screamed into the phone. "You've just complicated my career in this part of the world and probably put my life in jeopardy. I need to make some security precautions. What a mess you've made of my life, and I thought I was doing you a favor as a friend. A friend wouldn't ruin a man's life like that!" He slammed down the phone.

Shiloh felt sorry for him, but she also wondered what he was doing working with such a criminal. Maybe he was just as bad, she told herself. In any case, she thought the loss of this friend was worth the price to retrieve Rose's painting and successfully execute her first assignment.

....

The dinner that night was the best Shiloh had eaten in Prague. Adam and Jakup picked all their favorites from the menu. They both wanted Shiloh to try everything they loved. It was the only opportunity that she'd had to talk with them about their families, their careers with the military, and now their security work. They had kept a professional distance so as not to become in any way emotionally attached, as they had been trained. That would raise the risk of distraction—a risk they could never take. As time neared for their departure to the airport, Shiloh needed to use the restroom. Adam walked with her across the dining room and waited outside in an alcove.

Shiloh finished and was washing her hands at the sink when a tall redhead stepped to the next sink. Shiloh smiled at her in the mirror and it was over, instantly, silently, and bloodlessly.

Veronique signaled Sasha through her earpiece, "Ready."

While Shiloh had been enjoying her dinner, Veronique had scoped out the women's restroom. To her surprise, she had found that it had a translucent window with a small upholstered chair underneath. This gave her an impromptu plan. While she was alone in the restroom, she'd checked to be certain that it would open easily to the rear of the building. Sasha had confirmed that Shiloh's body could be lifted through the window and had put their car in place. Then they'd just had to hope that Shiloh would use the restroom before leaving the restaurant.

They put her into the trunk of their car and drove off into the night.

Adam felt that Shiloh had certainly had enough time. His internal alarm went off. He knocked on the women's room door and there was no answer. He burst in and checked every stall. They were empty. He spoke to Jakup on their com, "She's gone."

Jakup was by his side in an instant. They searched the men's room and the kitchen. Nothing! They found the rear exit door and searched the entire restaurant grounds. Again, nothing! They stood outside the back door and looked at each other. Adam spoke for both of them, "Two special forces professionals and we've lost her!"

They called central control and told them to notify the night security commander. Their focus was on Gustaf. He was now in the middle of their crosshairs.

For the next twenty-four hours, other members of their security team blanketed Prague in a comprehensive search. Every hospital, clinic, and morgue was visited, without a trace of Shiloh. Security at the airport had allowed them to review their footage. Bus terminals and train stations were checked. All to no avail. The owner of the security agency was an old friend of Harley's since his Mossad days. He would not let this go unresolved, and neither would Jakup and Adam.

EXECUTION

Lee bin Osman's airstrip was set in a picturesque plain between verdant hills and the winding Kinta River that flows through Ipoh. The tarmac had been cut cleanly through the green grassy plain and was lined with clusters of tall palm trees and leafy umbrella-like trees that shaded flowering shrubs. James would be landing in a tropical paradise.

A large white Mercedes was parked at the end of the strip, waiting for the jet as it taxied down the runway. As it pulled to a stop close to the car, a manservant stepped out of the passenger seat and approached the jet. Lee loved regimentation and luxury and had his staff dress accordingly. This man cut an imposing, almost regal figure in his fine cream-colored linen tunic and trousers. A handwoven black-and-cream sarong wrapped around his trim hips, and a black linen songkok, a truncated cone-shaped hat, was perched on his head. It looked to James like a panoramic scene from an imagined canvas or the opening wide shot for a film set in paradise.

"Welcome, Mr. Pfyffer." The manservant welcomed James with a waist-deep bow of respect as he stepped off the plane. "I'm here to take you to Mr. Bin Osman's home. Do you have any luggage you wish me to collect?"

"No, only a small crate in the cargo hold. Please handle it very carefully."

"I'll collect the crate immediately and most gently place it in the back of the car." He opened the rear door of the Mercedes for James, saying, "Please make yourself comfortable, sir; it's a short drive."

There were no words spoken on the way to the mansion, only the sound of a soft bowing violin coming through the car's speakers. The vegetation that surrounded the mansion was so thick that the manservant who opened the door for James to exit the car seemed to step out of a manicured jungle. Another servant opened the heavy, double-entry carved teak doors to welcome James. Each servant was dressed in the same elegant uniform and offered the same bow of respect. Two other servants gently retrieved the crate from the back of the car and carried it behind James into the mansion.

"Is this what I have to look forward to?" James wondered as he stepped across the marble floor of the cavernous entry. He felt like royalty as he followed yet another servant into a luxurious sitting room, which, unlike the other rooms, was furnished in a sleek, minimalist, postmodern style.

Drew, posing as Michael, stood alone in the room, patiently waiting for James. He was dressed in a long black silk tunic with no adornments. He wore his usual round wire-rimmed glasses, and his sandy-colored hair was cut a bit crisp for this occasion. He offered his hand to James.

"It is a pleasure to meet you, Mr. Pfyffer. I am Michael, Mr. Bin Osman's second-in-command. I am fully authorized to take care of this transaction, and I promise it will be completed very efficiently." He motioned to a servant, who approached carrying an open laptop. He handed it to Drew, who immediately turned the screen so James could see a banking statement with an easily read balance of €50 million. "This should assure you that the money is immediately available for the sale."

"This is really happening," James silently mused. He could barely contain himself.

"May we see the painting now, sir?"

"Yes, yes of course. Are your servants prepared to handle such a treasure?"

"You may be assured they are most competent." The crate had been resting on a large table that had obviously been placed in the room for this purpose, and an elegant easel was sitting next to it with proper viewing lights already placed. Two servants James had not already seen entered the room with the tools necessary to open the create and gloves to handle the painting. They made quick work of the uncrating and then proceeded to unwrap the painting. They clearly knew exactly what they were doing and the importance of this work of art. With gloved hands, they lifted the canvas onto the easel.

"Mr. Pfyffer—" Drew began.

"Please, call me James," he responded cordially—this man was about to give him €50 million, after all!

"James, Mr. Bin Osman insists that the art be verified by our expert before we complete the transaction. Only good business; I'm certain that you understand."

"Yes, of course. I have no doubt it can quickly be verified."

"Indeed, we've flown in an internationally respected postimpressionist expert for this authentication. Ms. Amy Fong from Hong Kong." With a nod from Drew, Amy was ushered into the room and without a word went straight to the painting and began her examination. Her gray chignon moved about as she studied the work.

"This has all been orchestrated, as if a scene in a play," thought James, his nerves beginning to fray. Fatigue from missed sleep on the long flight was beginning to get a grip on him, and he suddenly realized that Mr. Bin Osman's second-in-command had never offered him a seat. He'd been standing all this time.

"Mr. Pfyffer, may I offer you some tea so you can relax while Ms. Fong conducts her analysis?" Drew asked.

"Thanks, but I think I'll wait until we've finished." He was too nervous to swallow anything at that moment, but his legs were starting to feel like jelly and he felt a headache coming on. He moaned inwardly, saying to himself, "Please don't let it be a migraine. I've got to keep it together just a little longer; everything is at stake."

After about fifteen minutes, Amy began shaking her head. James assumed it was in appreciation of this masterpiece. She continued to peer at it intensely as she removed a jeweler's loop and examined the artwork inch by inch. After about an hour, she called Drew aside, saying, "I'd like to speak to you in private. Please."

They both stepped into a small side room where Max had been waiting and observing everything. Amy motioned for her to join them.

Amy said to both of them, "I stalled as long as I could to be convincing. I'm confused. What's going on? This painting is an obvious fake! And a not very good one at that."

"Are you 100 percent sure?" asked Max in total surprise.

"Yes. I have absolutely no doubt."

Drew pulled out his mobile and put it on speaker. "Ren, the painting is a fake! James is here alone; I don't know where Peter is."

There was a long silence on the other end of the line. Then Ren answered, "Drew, have a couple of Lee's security guys get out to the plane now and search it for any sign of Peter. See if the pilots know anything. If Peter's still in Paris, he must have the real Van Gogh. We need to know yesterday! Otherwise, stick with the script! Have the security team call and report to both of us directly from the plane to save time."

Drew opened the door and asked for two security men to come in immediately. They wore blue police uniforms with berets, rather than the visored caps worn by the police who were currently stationed around the mansion, awaiting his call to enter and arrest James. He would learn later that Lee's security men were a special branch of the regular police who were paid directly by the owners of the properties and the people they protected.

As soon as the security men had taken off for the plane in accordance with Drew's orders, Max spoke. She had been trying to stay out of the way, as she'd promised. "Well, at least we can still proceed with our plans to have him arrested, but for the moment only for fraud. It's a start, and I'm certain he'll be confessing to much more after he spends his first night in a Malaysian jail. I want to talk to him before we bring in the police. May I do that?"

"Of course, but let Amy and me go in first. It will make the impact all the greater if we give him Amy's report first."

"Got it," Max agreed, her eyes narrowed like a cat preparing to stalk its prey for the kill.

Drew and Amy returned to James, who was still waiting in the room with the fake Van Gogh, pacing like a caged animal. His temper was growing short, and he demanded, "What's going on?"

"I'm afraid, Mr. Pfyffer, you have brought Lee bin Osman a fake Van Gogh," Amy said with authority, "and a very poor one at that."

James was stunned. He froze where he stood. "What do you mean? It can't be," James stammered.

Just then, Max strode into the room. "Do you remember me, James? I certainly remember you, and I am so happy that the Malaysian police are in the house, waiting to arrest you at our signal. We thought

204

you'd be jailed for attempting to sell a stolen work of art. Now you'll be arrested for fraud, trying to sell a fake piece of art. Don't worry, that alone will get you at least ten years in a Malaysian jail before more charges are added." These words were said with great satisfaction and a wide smile.

"That is, unless you tell us where to find the real Van Gogh, and you agree to voluntary extradition to France to pay for your crimes." Max seemed out of breath as she spoke those last words. Her fury at James was unabated, and she almost hoped he'd not agree to be extradited to France, so he'd spend years suffering in a Malaysian prison.

While Max was venting her spleen at James, one of the security guards entered the room and handed Drew a mobile phone. The sight of a police uniform seemed to unhinge James. Without realizing that he was speaking out loud, James growled, "You SOB, Peter, you've put me in jail and just screwed me out of €50 million!" Then he muttered under his breath, "This has been a fiasco from the beginning."

"Well, James, you did it to yourself," Drew said, returning the mobile phone to the security guard. "You threw Peter and the painting off your plane in Paris. Your pilots just reported seeing Peter walking away on the tarmac with a duffle, likely carrying a rolled-up masterpiece worth over €100 million. You had it, James, and you threw it away."

Max broke out in a self-satisfying bout of laughter. "Well done, James. I had to pay a fortune to get back my family's Rembrandt that you stole. You used exactly the gambit to steal the Van Gogh, but I just got the first piece of my revenge. Priceless!"

Drew turned to the security guard and simply said, "We're ready." Within minutes, the regular police with their distinctive hats with visors entered the room from all directions.

The moment they put the handcuffs on James, he started yelling, "I want extradition. I want to go back to France. I'll admit everything, just let me go back. You can use my plane! Anything you want!"

Max, Amy, and Drew could hear his screams as the police practically carried him to an unmarked police van waiting outside. Max couldn't resist saying, "It's going to be a long, terrifying night for James; a good start!"

Chapter 12: CONFRONTATION

The moment Ren and the team got the call from the security detail in James's plane, they left en masse for Peter's flat. Now that they knew for certain that Peter had the original, Ren hoped the presence of the team might intimidate Peter and entice him to give up the location of the Van Gogh more readily. Also working for them would be a lot of bad news they were bringing to share with him from Malaysia.

When they got to Peter's door, Ren pulled out his mobile to see if by any miracle the Q-bug, the voice-activated transmitter Alex had planted earlier, was still transmitting, and it was. Ren could clearly hear on his mobile that Peter was talking to someone. Harley banged on the door and called out, "Peter, we can hear you. The whole SALT team is here and we're not going away. If you don't let us in, we'll force our way in."

Moments passed, and Harley was about to put his body to the door when Peter called to them. "Come in," he said, "it's unlocked."

They found him standing in the middle of his living room, dressed as always in his distinctive professorial tweeds, tie in place. He had drawn his short, portly frame up straight and tall, much as an animal raises its body hairs to appear larger and more ferocious to a predator.

Ren moved across the space aggressively and came to stand toe to toe with Peter. "A fake, you made a fake! James just flew all the way to Malaysia thinking that he had the real Van Gogh to sell! But you want to hear the bad news?"

Peter was breathing now as if he'd been running, but he said nothing and stood motionless.

"We set a trap, and James flew right into it and now he's sitting in a Malaysian prison, squealing like a pig, begging for extradition. Trying to sell a fake masterpiece can get you into a whole heap of trouble in that part of the world. All the bloody details of your plan are coming out. You're going to prison for a long time, Peter, and worse if they throw an accomplice-to-murder charge at you."

Tears started to fill Peter's eyes and slowly roll down his plump cheeks. "I never ... I never meant for anyone to be hurt. It was going to be one last job with James so I could stop all this. I lost everything a long time ago. I wanted one more chance to find a way out, and when Max gave Dean my name and he called, I thought this was that chance. It just went all wrong. You've got to believe me; it was only about money."

"Then make it right now, for the Martines. Tell us where the Van Gogh is so we can return it to them." Ren's voice got louder as he yelled at Peter with pure passion in his voice. "Do this one right thing in your life, Peter, do a decent honorable thing if the world of art ever truly meant anything to you."

Peter's breathing became more forced and he suddenly sank into the armchair next to him. He started weeping softly. "Yes, yes, I do care. You're right." Before he could utter another word, a look of horror came over his face. His mouth gaped open, and he grabbed his head with both hands as if to stop something from falling out. His elbow slipped off the arm of the chair and he slumped over the side, motionless.

208

Harley stepped forward and yelled, "Get him on the floor! I think he's having a stroke." His experience with Mossad took over.

Ren and Harley eased him to the floor. Kat punched in 112 to call for help as Ren pulled Peter into his arms and spoke into his ear, "Peter, help is on the way, hang on."

"He's breathing, but barely; he's not going to make it."

"Peter, where did you put the Van Gogh? Please, it'll be lost again, this time forever. Peter, where is it?" Holding Peter tighter into his arms, his ear pressed against his lips, Ren heard something, but he couldn't make it out for sure. "Peter, are you saying poppy, like the flower?" He never got a response; Peter was gone.

The rest of the team were kneeling and standing around Ren and Peter. Alex spoke first. "This isn't what any of us wanted. Would he be alive now if we hadn't confronted him?" The sound of sirens could be heard in the distance, growing closer by the minute.

The least emotional member of the team, Harley got off his knees, put his arm around Alex, and responded, "You saw the color of his face when we opened the door. He was a heart attack or stroke waiting to happen. I think he knew that his days were numbered, and he was hanging on to keep the Van Gogh out of James's hands above all else."

"Thanks for that, Harley," Alex replied. "At least it helps to think that right now." Just as she finished speaking, an ambulance crew appeared at the door and suddenly there was a crowd of people in the room. The SALT team told the crew what had happened with Peter, then backed away to let them do their job, which wasn't much now.

As they worked, Alex went to stand next to Ren and whispered, "I retrieved the hidden Q-bug." He gave her a nod of thanks.

209

It wasn't long before Detective Arnot arrived at the flat. Ren had called him as soon as the ambulance had arrived. He had simply said, "I think you should be here now. We're all at Peter Meier's flat." He disconnected before the detective could ask any questions. He'd rather handle that in person.

Wherever Detective Arnot had been when he got the call, he seemed to get there in no time. He walked into the flat and took a look around, and Ren swore that he saw steam coming off the top of his head. "This isn't going to be easy," he thought, making his way across the room to the detective.

"What have you done? I trusted you."

"We learned that James and Peter were going to make a run for it with the art, and we had to act fast, more quickly than I thought you could with all the red tape you'd have to deal with. James is sitting in a Malaysian jail in Ipoh begging for you to extradite him.

"He's giving up everything—singing like a bird, as we say. Unfortunately, the painting he had to sell was a fake, so the base charge they arrested him on is fraud. Turns out he threw Peter off the plane here, without knowing that he had the real Van Gogh in his duffle. So we still don't have the painting, and Peter's dead. It looked like a stroke to us. He actually died in my arms."

"Well, you blew it," Detective Arnot growled. "Maybe there is some justice after all. You still don't have the art, and no idea where it is. Peter's dead, so we can't make a deal with him to find the art." He motioned to two policemen standing in the room and told them, "Go through those crates, but open them very carefully. There may be a multimillion-euro painting in one of them. We need to look at every painting you find." Not wanting to be on the receiving end of Detective Arnot's anger, they quickly moved to the crates and gingerly began opening them. Peter had obviously been doing some of the crating himself and had left his tools lying about.

"Detective Arnot, I know that I broke our agreement, but the sooner you get the extradition process going at this end, the sooner you'll have the theft and murder case solved. James is one broken man at the moment, one very frightened man."

Detective Arnot glared at Ren and stepped away, pulling out his mobile and turning away so Ren could not hear his conversation.

There were only five crates, so it didn't take too long to get them all open. Before them sat five pieces of abstract art. Detective Arnot turned to look at the art as he continued his conversation and nodded his understanding: the Van Gogh was not there.

Chapter 13: FINDING POPPY

The team returned to the hotel and gathered in Ren and Alex's suite. Ren had talked to Drew on the way back, updating him on Peter's death, his conversation with Detective Arnot, and the clue "poppy" so Drew could start digging from his end.

"Why didn't you tell Detective Arnot about Peter's last word?" Kat asked.

Ren answered, "I think we need to find the Van Gogh ourselves. Peter's last word was a clue, and I'd rather not have it tangled up and lost in the police bureaucracy."

"But we have no idea what 'poppy' means. Maybe a Parisian might understand it," Kat said, not convinced of the wisdom of withholding that information from Detective Arnot.

Alex and Harley were silent, lost in their own internet searches. Then Harley said, "Peter must have mistrusted James very early on. Otherwise, why have a copy made?"

Kat added, "And you can't have a copy made overnight either. Peter must have ordered it as soon as the original was hijacked. Then, when he and James decided to cut and run, he crated the copy and rolled the original and put it in his duffel."

"It's not in his apartment. He must have hidden it on his way back from Le Bourget Airport, after James ordered him out of the plane. That means it would still

213

be rolled in some sort of tube and may still be in the duffel. We have a limited area to concentrate on," Harley said, turning his laptop for everyone to see the map he'd pulled up of the greater Paris area.

"He'd have hidden it where it'd be safe for a long time, in case he was caught. And it must be somewhere no one could accidentally find it, in a safe environment from the weather," Alex added.

"Great thoughts, but where?" Ren asked. "I'm guessing that any tube big enough to hold the canvas with some protective wrapping and fit into a large duffel would be about three feet long. So we have a rough idea of the needed dimensions of a hiding place, with and without the duffel.

"Kat, you said a minute ago that a Parisian might understand what 'poppy' means. I think I know just where to go for help." Ren picked up his mobile, searched his contacts, and put in a call. "May I please speak to Thomas Pfyffer? This is Ren Merit calling."

A few minutes later, he finished the call. "Thomas will see me now. He had said to ask if we ever needed help, and we need help now. He also needs to be told about James and Peter. So I'm off. You guys keep digging, and I'll call as soon as I'm finished. Say your prayers, everybody, we need a miracle right now, the Martines need a miracle."

....

Ren was taken directly to Thomas's office. It reeked of history. Generations of Pfyffers had occupied this space, which was lined with leather-bound volumes, probably many first additions, and masculine, well-worn leather furniture that was beautifully polished with age. Magnificent oriental carpets were spread over wide-planked hand-cut wooden floors teased to a beautiful patina. Thomas had replaced his formal suit coat with a hand-knit cashmere sweater colored in a

214

subtle pattern that brought the Alps to mind. Ren knew that beneath the elegant exterior, Thomas carried heavy responsibilities on his shoulders, and the news Ren brought with him would only add to that weight.

There was a tea set on a low oval table in front of the fireplace. Thomas seated them in two large wingback chairs on either side of it. "Ren, do you care to join me for some tea?"

Thinking that joining him might give Thomas some comfort as he delivered the news about Peter, Ren answered, "Yes, black please."

Thomas handed Ren his cup. "We're not the sort of men who dally. Please ..." In that one word, Thomas gave him permission to dive right in.

"This morning, Peter passed away in my arms. We believe at this point it was a stroke. I am so very sorry for your loss."

Thomas put his cup back into its saucer and set it on the tray. He put one elbow on the arm of his chair and placed his hand under his chin, starring into the cold, empty fireplace. Ren sat quietly and just let him be with his thoughts.

After a few minutes, Thomas began to speak slowly, as if from a foggy distance. "When you said the words, my first thoughts went immediately to my last conversation with Peter. I told you about it at our last meeting. He pushed me away out of shame for his actions, and I let it end there. Yes, I tried to say it didn't matter to me, but how hard did I really try? We lost all those years we could have shared together. I never before and have not since experienced another friendship like it. Close, meaningful friendships, especially between men, don't happen that often, at least for me. Peter and I had that, and I let it go. We both let it go, and now he's gone."

Removing his hand from his chin and folding his hands together in his lap, Thomas turned to Ren. "Thank you for coming and telling me, Ren. Somehow it helps to know that you were with him at that moment."

"My team and I were all there in his flat. We had just gotten word about James. This part is in some ways more difficult to tell you. We had suspicions about your brother's involvement in the Van Gogh theft, and I'm sorry to report that those suspicions proved to be well founded. They also led us to discovering Peter's part in the crime. But we needed to catch James and Peter together with the painting, and so we set up a trap and James walked right into it.

"There's no easy way to say this, Thomas, and as you say, men like us get to the point. James has been arrested in Ipoh, Malaysia, and is begging for extradition to France. He flew to Malaysia to sell the Van Gogh for €50 million. The sale was all arranged by us. But to our shock, as well as James's, when our expert examined the art, we all learned together that it was a fake. From your pilots, we immediately learned that before they took off from La Bourget, they saw Peter walking away from your plane with a large duffle. James had thrown him off the plane, thinking that he still had the original on board. Peter had made a fake. So after we received a call this morning with this information, we went immediately to Peter, knowing that he must have the painting. He admitted everything, but he died before he could tell us where he hidden the real Van Gogh." Ren stopped. He had just unloaded a lifetime's worth of pain on Thomas, and the man deserved a moment to process it.

Thomas had gotten up as Ren was telling the tale, and now he walked over to look out one of the windows behind his desk, almost as if he were unconsciously seeking a barrier between himself and Ren's words.

Thomas stood motionless at the windows for a while. "James," he thought, "I'm sorry. Sorry for all the years I let you get away with your petty acts of

216

selfishness. I allowed them to grow into monstrous acts of cunning that brought huge financial losses to me and the company. I am your brother and I let it all happen unpunished. I wanted to believe that you would somehow change, and now this. You've gone too far. You are beyond my reach."

At last he turned and spoke aloud to Ren, "I was not aware of any of this, Ren, I can assure you. But I was aware of the man my brother had become. He has walked off the plank this time. If it's possible, I'd like to ask that my brother not be extradited until he has admitted everything. There are monies missing from our company, and I'm certain he has them hidden in offshore accounts. People's jobs, their livelihoods, depend on us. The company is on the verge of ruin. He has stolen not only the Van Gogh but our future. He couldn't even be honorable with Peter, an old friend and his partner in crime. I believe my brother is a psychopath. There is probably no hope for him, but I must try to repair his path of destruction in any way I can. Again I say to you, how can I help?"

"I will let Detective Arnot know of your wish concerning the extradition. I know that he'll appreciate your cooperation and be in touch with you. But there is something we need your help with, although we know it's a long shot. It's about Peter. As he died, he was trying to tell us where the painting is hidden. He said a word that sounded like 'poppy,' but we don't know what he meant. As our team talked this morning, we wondered if a native French speaker, especially someone close to Peter, could help us, and that brought me here to you.

"We know he must have had the art in his duffel, and he didn't have much time to find a place to hide it safely. So we believe it's likely somewhere between Le Bourget Airport and his apartment. The police searched his apartment this morning and it is not there."

217

Thomas's eyes lit up, and a faint smile crept out across his lips as if he'd just received a small piece of hope in the midst of all this heaviness. "I think I can help, but I need you to take a ride with me. Let me get my car, and I'll explain more on the road." Thomas went to his desk, called his driver, and asked him to bring his car around.

"I need to let my team know I won't be back for a while," said Ren. "Please excuse me for a minute."

"Of course. I'll meet you at the front entrance as soon as you're finished. I would have suggested that your team join us, but I think this matter is best handled by just the two of us. Perhaps they can join us a bit later if we have some good luck." Thomas took his suit coat out of the closet and left his office to Ren.

Alex picked up on the first ring. "Ren, any good news for us yet?"

"You picked the right word, Alex. I just finished a long conversation with Thomas, bringing him up to date on all that's happened in the last few hours. I'll fill you all in soon, but what's important now is that he reacted positively to the word 'poppy' and said that he thinks he can help us. All I can tell you right now is we're just about to leave the office in his car, and he's promised to tell me more as we drive. He felt that we should do this alone, just the two of us, and that perhaps you three could join us later if things go well. I don't have the foggiest idea, Alex, but we'll know soon. Keep those prayers coming, maybe they're working. You might want to give Drew an update. He's probably still in Ipoh with Max. Otherwise, sit tight."

"Got it." Alex had Ren on speaker, and Harley said, "You have us on the edge of our seats, man," while Kat added, "Bring home that miracle, Ren."

"Will do," he answered with a hopeful smile on his face as he walked outside and joined Thomas at his car.

218

....

As they made their way through Paris traffic, Thomas began to speak. "Remember when we last met, I told you about the lovely weekends Peter and I used to share at his place in the country?"

"Yes, of course."

"Well, it's in a small village called Bonneuil-en-France, usually referred to as just Bonneuil. Its population is about a few hundred – or was when I last visited; it's probably grown since then. And it's very close to Le Bourget Airport."

"I see, very interesting," replied Ren.

"It gets better. Peter was raised in this village. He was the only child of a couple who were teachers. They raised him at a very early age to have a great love and appreciation for all things literary and artistic. Needless to say, not the typical upbringing for the children of this small village at the time."

Ren could tell they were driving away from the center of Paris. The neighborhoods were changing as the shops became smaller, and the large apartment buildings were giving way to townhouses and smaller apartment structures. "Are we by any chance headed to Bonneuil?"

"We are indeed, and we'll be there very soon; it's only about thirteen kilometers from the center of Paris. I'd leave the office early on a Friday, when I was lucky enough to have a weekend free, and get to Peter's in time to share a glass of his favorite wine of the week. We'd relax under the shade of his chestnut trees until it was time for us to start preparing dinner. Always simple fare with the freshest ingredients from the local farmers, depending on the time of year, of course." As if reliving the moments, Thomas sighed. "Nothing like the posh gourmet meals in the city, but somehow better. I think we cooked with our hearts. It was wonderful," he said with a touch of nostalgia..

219

"Sounds perfect, Thomas. I can't say that I've ever shared quite that same experience with a male friend—or with a female friend, for that matter." He could imagine him and Shiloh sharing such an experience and longed for the opportunity. "Soon, I hope," he said to himself.

"I'm sorry, I digress. Peter had a rather idyllic life until the age of thirteen, when both his parents were killed in a traffic accident. Their car was hit by a large commercial truck that had lost its brakes. To say that it was a tragic accident seems to understate its toll. I'm sure the driver never recovered from it; there was absolutely nothing he could have done to prevent it, but it took two lives and that is never forgotten. As I will never forget the death of our van's guard—and now I know that whatever happened to him happened in a hijacking arranged by my brother out of his own selfish greed."

"What happened to Peter after their death. Did he have any other family?"

"That was one blessing to come out of this tragedy. His mother had a brother, Gabriel Bernard, who had been very close to Peter since his birth. He never married and had no children of his own. He moved into Peter's family home when the courts gave him full custody of Peter. Gabriel worked as an accountant in that region until he retired. He shared the same passion for learning as his sister had, and so Peter's opportunities for learning never lost a beat. When Peter moved to Paris to pursue his career in the art world, he never failed to return to Gabriel and the house in Bonneuil at every opportunity. Gabriel, or Poppi, as Peter always called him, was his touchstone, his father and mother. Gabriel, that beautiful man, gave Peter every ounce of his love and compassion. That's where Peter got his compassion from. I know it's probably impossible for you to imagine him that way, but that was the true Peter. That's what got him into

220

trouble and cost him his career, as I've already told you. He was trying to help a friend.

"Now you understand why I reacted to the word 'Poppi' back in my office. If there is anyone Peter would have trusted with the Van Gogh, it would be Gabriel—Poppi. I'm hoping he still lives in the same house. I honestly could not remember the address, but I will never forget how to get there. In a few minutes we'll know if he's still there and if he has the Van Gogh."

"Quite a story, quite a life," said Ren. "It makes sense that in his dying breath that is the word, or I should say the name, that Peter worked so desperately to make me hear when I asked where the painting was. We didn't think at all about it being a name. We were thinking only of the English word for the flower."

"I understand, but a Frenchman would immediately think 'grandfather.' Gabriel was some years older than his sister—Peter's mother—and he felt more like a grandfather than an uncle to Peter as a young boy. It was my first thought, but I couldn't tell you where to find the house. We needed to find it together. Besides, I am so grateful to have an excuse to return and to hopefully see Bernard."

They drove in silence for the remaining few miles, with traffic thinning out as they got farther from the heart of Paris. Eventually they reached the town and Thomas began to try to find his way 'home.'

He found the streets much the same and after a few missed cues, he pulled into the driveway of an old stone cottage. To Ren it looked like something out of a travel magazine promoting stays in a French cottage in the woods. Lush trees surrounded the cottage, and the front garden was filled with beautiful flowers. Again his thoughts drifted to Shiloh. "She'd love this," he thought. "We'd probably never want to leave."

"Well, this is it. The front door is open, so somebody's home, and the gardens are as lovingly cared for as I remember." Thomas looked at Ren.

"Whatever we find, I'm glad I've come and I'm glad you're here with me. Let's go find Poppi and hopefully the Van Gogh." He smiled at Ren warmly and then turned to get out of the car, and Ren followed.

Thomas stood at the open door and called first "Gabriel" and then "Poppi." Before long an elderly gentleman, a little portly like Peter and wearing the same wire-rimmed glasses, came to the door. He was dressed in softly worn trousers, a plaid shirt, and a beret atop his balding head. It took him only a moment to recognize Thomas. "Thomas, is it really you? It's been so very long." He took Thomas in his arms and embraced him as a son, tears in his eyes. He stepped back just far enough to pull a handkerchief out of his pocket and wipe his eyes. "Sorry. Please introduce me to this nice-looking young man."

"Poppi, this is Ren Merit, a friend. We've come to share some news with you. Can we come in?" Poppi smiled as he heard the name Ren Merit.

"Of course, Thomas. This is your home; you are always welcome. Why don't we find a shady spot in the garden out back, where you and Peter always loved to sit and talk. When I saw you, I hoped perhaps that you and Peter would have come together. He was just here, you know." They all took a seat under one of the chestnut trees. "Oh, may I offer you something cool to drink, or a glass of wine, perhaps?"

"Maybe a bit later, Poppi. I have something important to share with you, and you know that Peter and I always liked to get things said without delay."

"I think he got that from me; accountants don't tarry."

"No doubt, Poppi. Is it all right that I still call you Poppi?"

"Of course, Thomas. You are like a brother to Peter and a son to me. I love to hear you say it. Yes indeed." He took both of Thomas's hands in his.

"Poppi, Ren just brought me some news before we left my office to find you. My heart breaks to tell you that early this morning Peter died of what we believe was a stroke. Ren was with him and can assure you that he went quickly and didn't suffer. His last word was your name, Poppi. I think it will be comforting to you, as it was to me, to hear that he died in Ren's arms. He wasn't alone."

Poppi leaned back in his chair, wrapping his arms around his body as best he could to comfort himself. Thomas pulled his own chair closer and wrapped his own arms around Poppi. The older man rested his head on Thomas's shoulder as he began to weep softly. "Oh Thomas, I am so grateful that you are the one to bring the news and to have you here just now with me. If I'd only known when Peter stopped yesterday that it would be the last time I'd ever see him, what would I have said? What should I have said? It's all I can think of right now. He was as a son to me. It should have been me, not Peter. He's still ... he was too young for this."

Thomas pulled out his own handkerchief and handed it to Poppi. "I know, Poppi. I have regrets too."

Ren left them together in the garden and headed for the kitchen he'd seen as they'd passed through the house. He wanted to get them both some water. He also wanted to give them a bit of time to grieve together in private. He took his time returning to the garden.

When Ren returned, he offered water to each of them. They both sipped a bit before putting their glasses down. Poppi seemed to have recovered somewhat and was trying to compose himself. Thomas spoke first: "Poppi, you said that Peter had just been here. Did he just stop by to check on you, or was there something special he wanted?"

"He came to leave something with me," answered Poppi, blowing his nose gently into the linen handkerchief. "He had stopped on his way home from Le Bourget to bring it to me. He had his duffel with him and told me that he had planned a trip but that it had been canceled at the last moment. I asked him what it was he wanted to leave with me. He said it would be better for me not to know, that he just wanted to leave it in his room until he came back to collect it or until a Ren Merit came to ask for it." Poppi looked Ren straight in the eyes when he said this. "Do you know what this is about, Ren?"

"Yes, I think so. Could you show us what Peter left for me?"

"I haven't seen it. I don't know what it is. Can you both come to Peter's room with me?"

Thomas and Ren followed Poppi to a bedroom at the back of the house. "This is Peter's room. He carried his duffel in here, but I didn't come with him. Since I don't see it anywhere, I assume he put it in his secret place. He loved putting special treasures in it, ever since he was a young boy. First it was pretty pebbles, then a special book or picture. Thomas, if you go to the panel just behind Peter's desk … you'll have to pull out his desk a bit." Thomas did just that. "Now push on the left side of the panel and it will swing out." As Thomas did that, the panel swung open. "Peter's dad made it for him when he was about six. He put hinges on it to make it work easily. At that age, Peter could crawl into it and hide—oh how he loved to do that!"

When the panel was fully open, they could all see the duffle standing on end. Thomas carefully pulled it out, knowing what was likely inside. He took it to Peter's bed and laid it down. "Ren, I think that you should do the honors. He left it for you."

Ren sat down on the bed next to the bag and unzipped it. At first, he saw only neatly folded clothes, but on top of them was an envelope with his name written on it. Poppi took a seat in a chair next to Peter's bed and said, "He asked me for an envelope and writing paper before he took the bag to his room. I guess that's when he wrote the note."

Ren opened the unsealed envelope and unfolded the single sheet of paper. He read it first to himself and then aloud to Thomas and Poppi. He was clearly overwhelmed by the message.

Ren,

If you're reading this, it means I've been jailed or worse. After James threw me off his plane earlier today, I decided that I couldn't take any more chances. I believe he is capable of anything.

I assume I have told you it was here, and I'm grateful that you've come. The most important thing at this point is to return the original Van Gogh to the Martine family. They will then have it to auction for its true value or keep for themselves. Pfyffer and Sons Insurance has lost its right to the work, since James organized the hijacking, and I played my part by bringing the opportunity to him. When I learned that the guard had been killed in the hijacking, I was terrified. I realized that I could be charged with accessory to murder or maybe worse, all because I had wanted one last opportunity to have a comfortable life for Poppi and me. I am mortified and heartbroken that Poppi will come to know all this. I hope that I might still have the opportunity to ask his forgiveness.

Returning the art to the Martines means at least I, with your help, will have made that possible. Art has been my whole world, Ren, and I suspect it has been a very important part of yours. You created SALT to recover lost treasures for people, and in the case of the Vatican, for many millions of people. Great art treasures are to be shared, and I hope that the Martines will decide to auction the work and that it ends up available for viewing by people all over the world in a great house like the Louvre or the Metropolitan.

Thank you for your help, Ren. I think that in a different time and circumstance, we might well have been friends, as Thomas and I once were. He was like a brother...

Peter Meier

Thomas had taken a seat on the bed on the opposite end of the bag as Ren read the letter aloud. All three men sat there in silence and let Peter's words wash over them like a cold shower, followed by a long, warm rinse that left them feeling sated, a bit dizzy, and drained of energy. Peter had taken them on a journey of his heart, and it was heavy and yet celebratory because in the end Peter had done the right thing … he had made it right for all three of them.

"I think it's time to open the painting," Ren said at last as he started removing the clothing from the bag. Thomas joined him and they both handed the clothes to Poppi, who took them into his hands as if they were pieces of his beloved Peter. They were all he had of him at the moment. They quickly came to a long piece of PVC pipe that had been cradled in the middle of the clothing to give it cushion. Ren carefully removed it from its nest, and Thomas moved the bag from the bed. Ren removed a cap Peter had placed on the end of the pipe and began to slowly pull out the rolled-up canvas. It was wrapped in acid-free paper to help protect it. Ren laid the canvas down on the bed, and he and Thomas slowly unrolled the paper and canvas and left it unfurled on the bed. Then they carefully lifted the paper to expose the painting. Ren let out an audible sigh of relief as he first saw the colors on the canvas— the same palette of colors he'd seen in Dean's photograph taken when he first discovered it.

"Yes," he finally said aloud as the entire canvas was revealed, "we've got it at last." It was unmistakably a Van Gogh. Poppi pulled his chair closer to have a better view and to hear Ren more clearly as he recounted the story of its discovery at the Martines' farmhouse, starting with Juliette's diary.

"What a beautiful journey this work has taken all these many years," Thomas said in a reverent voice. "And to have the diary to walk the viewer through the journey of its creation is a priceless gift to all of us. Like

Peter, I hope one day I can stand at the Louvre and read the pages of the diary in full while gazing at this work on the wall. If it's the Metropolitan, then you and I will go there, Poppi. I know I'm dreaming, but this painting deserves another miracle, wouldn't you say?" Both men agreed, their silent responses written on their tear-stained faces.

"Ren, the rest of your team should be here with us at this moment. Poppi, do you think that you and I, with a little help from Ren, could put together a French country feast of celebration in the garden tonight? As we often did with Peter?"

"I know that nothing would make Peter happier tonight," responded Poppi. "We'll make a menu and do a little shopping in the village before everybody closes up for the night."

"Perfect, Poppi. I think it's best to leave the painting unrolled so the rest of the team can see it when they arrive, and then we'll roll it again and put it back in the tube," Ren said. "Now I'll call the team and get them on the road."

"Poppi and I will check the kitchen to see what we need for this feast," Thomas added.

FEAST

Thomas and Poppi purchased two chickens at the butcherie. While the butcher dismembered the birds for the sauté pan, they tasted and then selected some cheese to add to the beautiful Roquefort Poppi had at home. This late in the day, they were lucky to snag one of the last round loaves of country bread at the small market. They also found some beautiful leeks, endive, and fingerling potatoes just in from a nearby farm. They piled their treasure into Thomas's car with satisfaction.

When Kat, Harley, and Alex arrived in a chauffeured "black car," the generic name given to private car services in Paris, the kitchen was already starting to smell glorious. They carried in the treats they'd found at a gourmet food shop near the hotel. In addition to the wine Ren had requested when he'd called, they'd brought some wonderful pâté they'd sampled at the shop, along with two baguettes for spreading and the pièce de résistance, luscious chocolate truffles from Belgium. With their two brimming baskets in hand, Ren marched them proudly into the kitchen, where aproned Thomas and Poppi greeted them as if they were family.

As soon as everyone had been introduced, Harley asked. "Do you think the four of us might take a moment to visit the Van Gogh?"

"Of course," Poppi replied. "Please, Ren take them into the bedroom so they can feast their eyes on the treasure they've been seeking. Thomas and I will unpack all the goodies and have the pâté and champagne ready when you return."

A minute later, the four of them stood like an honor guard beside the Van Gogh lying before them on the bed.

"What do you think?" asked Ren.

"It's spectacular! I think I'd begun to wonder if it really existed after the forgery was revealed in Ipoh," answered Kat.

"Well, we did it again. By hook or by crook, as my grandfather used to tell us. Just when it looked bleakest, here it is," said Harley.

Alex chuckled. "And none of us will ever forget the French endearment for grandfather . . ."

"P-O-P-P-I," they all chimed in to spell it out loud.

Ren pulled out the letter Peter had written to him and handed it to them to read. Kat took it and read it aloud. When she finished, they were all obviously moved by Peter's words.

"It's a beautiful confession of a fine soul in the end," said Alex. "Ren, are you going to leave it with

229

Poppi? It seems fitting, don't you think? Even though it was addressed to you?"

"Absolutely, it is indeed his to keep. I'll give it to him as we leave. Kat, will you do the honors and help me roll this back up and put it in the tube? I'll see that Detective Arnot gets it in the morning so that it goes through the proper chain of command before it's returned to the Martines. I'll also call Dean and give him the good news, and of course Max! Without her, we wouldn't be here on so many levels."

"I think we have many toasts to make tonight!" Alex added. "We'll called Drew and give him the great news!"

"Well, this wasn't the celebration I had planned for us, but I think it might turn out to be one of the most special we've ever shared." A spontaneous SALT team hug followed.

....

The chilled Veuve Clicquot was carefully uncorked. While Harley enjoyed his sparkling Perrier and everyone else sipped their champagne, they worked on their kitchen tasks, slathering the soft rich pâté onto slices of baguette. All hands were now on deck and the warm aromas of the kitchen conjured up everyone's childhood memories of home, real or imagined. Poppi's chicken and potatoes with chopped garlic and tarragon from his garden sizzled in rich duck fat as Kat observed over his shoulder. "The fat makes all the difference, Kat," he told her. "You wait and see, you're going to love the taste." He smiled warmly as he said the words, just now at a loss to express his comfort at their presence, at this whole wonderful scene in his usually empty kitchen.

Kat had already prepared the endive and Roquefort salad, as Poppi had instructed. Harley assembled the cheese and fruit platter for dessert. To the Rochebaron, a soft blue cheese, and the Saint

Albray, similar to a Camembert but less intense, he added sliced apples and small bunches of green table grapes from Poppi's wooden fruit bowl.

Thomas prepared his grandmother's leeks in another sauté pan, starting with sweet butter and adding lardons—small pieces of chopped bacon—with sea salt and ground pepper, then the sliced leeks with just a light touch of honey. To no one in particular, he said, "I hope I've remembered my grand-mère's recipe correctly."

Harley paused in his labors and leaned over to peer into the pan. "Thomas, it looks wonderful. I'll put my money on you," and they both chuckled. "I'll take it," Thomas replied, looking at this young man and trying to imagine James ever caring to pause long enough to savor such a simple but lovingly prepared food.

Ren had been assigned table duty and had set the long table on the small terrace at the back of the house under a trellis of grapevines. He had found everything he needed in the dining room to set a perfect country table, complete with a large blue-patterned linen tablecloth with matching napkins, white stoneware, candles for the table, and lanterns for the terrace and garden beyond. Alex joined him to help finish up. After she'd worked by his side for a while, she looked up and said, "Ren, thank you for this. I can't imagine a more perfect ending, a more perfect celebration. To find myself here in this family home in France tonight … I just don't have the words."

Ren understood her emotional reaction; he had experienced it earlier. "I'm right there with you, Alex," he said, giving her a brotherly hug. "It's been quite a day. We could never have imagined this morning in Peter's flat that tonight we'd be sharing a meal with his Poppi and Thomas. The world is full of surprises, isn't it?"

They stood together for a while, deep in their own thoughts, until Alex stirred herself and barked, "Okay, back to work! The food is coming ..."

Everyone pitched in to deliver the large platters and bowls of food to the table. The bottles of Joseph Drouhin Côte de Beaune were uncorked, the large crusty loaf of bread was sliced, and just before everyone settled in to enjoy the feast, Thomas proposed a toast to honor the recovery of the Van Gogh, and to Peter. "How Peter would have loved this night. I believe that he is somewhere in the stars, enjoying us enjoying this table and so relieved that the Van Gogh will soon be in its rightful place."

The sound of good conversation drifted out into the garden throughout the evening. Strangers becoming good friends, good friends and colleagues becoming a more closely knit family. Before everyone became too sated, Harley passed the platter of cheese and fruit and Ren uncorked a Sancerre Rouge that Poppi had chosen from his own wine collection and particularly liked to share with his cheeses. Everyone felt as deliciously rich as the cheeses they were enjoying. The evening was winding down, as was all their energy. It had been a very long day for all of them.

Harley left the table and returned with the box of truffles and opened them with a flourish. "Something to give us just enough energy to finish a wonderful night, one I personally shall never forget. Poppi, may I thank you from the bottom of my heart," he added, passing the box to him for first choice.

Thomas got up suddenly. "I think we need some expresso to enjoy with these fine chocolates."

"We'll help!" Alex said as she and Kat joined him as he headed for the kitchen.

Ren, in a very contemplative mood, turned to Poppi and said softly, "You couldn't know, but I lost my parents at thirty-one in a similar accident to Peter's folks. I wasn't as young as Peter, but it was a tremendous loss to me. You can't imagine what I would have given to have had someone like you in my life, Poppi. It would have meant everything and more. What you gave Peter was incalculable. I held him at the end, and his one word was Poppi. He came to you for help in the end. You were home, trust, love." Poppi came to Ren, and Ren stood to let Poppi take him in his arms, like a father. The two stood together, holding each other as a son holds his father.

.....

Harley had called the "black car" driver to pick them up. The beautiful evening had come to an end. Thomas had decided to spend the night and was standing at the door with Poppi to say good night. There were caring words shared with the goodbyes.

Poppi gave everyone hugs as they departed. "Say hello to Christopher for me, Kat. Whatever you decide will be the right decision I'm sure." He wished Harley and Alex safe travels and to Ren said, "I'm so happy that you found Shiloh. I hope that one day you might bring her to visit me."

"Just one more thing, Poppi," Ren said as he placed Peter's letter in his hands, "I think this is yours to keep. The police may need to borrow it for a while as evidence, but if so Detective Arnot will make certain that it comes back to you."

Tears streaming down his wrinkled cheeks, Poppi hugged Ren and then kissed him on both checks. "Thank you. Thank you, for everything." Thomas stood behind Poppi and nodded his head in agreement.

And the evening was over.

....

On the way back to Paris, Ren got a call from Drew, who was still in Malaysia. "Ren, I don't know how to say this ..." His voice broke with emotion.

"What is it, Drew, are you there? Are you okay? Has something happened to you?"

"Shiloh is gone."

EPILOGUE

At the trial, James testified against Victor and, in a bid for a lighter sentence, also provided a list of his numbered bank accounts, which included money taken from Pfyffer and Sons Insurance. The Martines would return the €10 million in insurance money to the company once the art was sold. This all gave Thomas Pfyffer a lot of money, more than enough to keep the company going. Wisely though, he realized he could never recover from the scandal and closed Pfyffer and Sons Insurance.

THE AUCTION

It was one year since the recovery of the lost Van Gogh. It had been authenticated by the Van Gogh Museum and returned to the Martines. The auction was held in London and drew a large bidding audience, both present in the auction room and in remote locations around the world. The Martine family was in attendance along with Max, Ren, and Dean. Max was registered as a qualified bidder.

The painting was hung on a wall panel that rotated into the room to reveal the work. The auctioneer approached his podium at the appointed time; his assistants on phones and computers were lined up against the wall to his left.

"Ladies and gentlemen, welcome. We are here to auction the new-to-market Vincent van Gogh painting entitled Stormy Day in the Olive Grove. But before we proceed, I am going to set aside tradition and read a short quotation from Vincent van Gogh to his brother Theo. This letter is well documented. Van Gogh speaks to his brother about this painting. Its location was unknown until a year ago."

He read:

Dearest Theo,

As I wrote you about my painting "Starry Night" as my view of the night scene from my prisonlike window here in Saint-Rémy, the good news is that I have just completed another painting, "Stormy Day in the Olive Grove." As much as I was displeased with my first painting, I wanted to paint something from my earlier days in Arles. I fell in love with the beautiful old and gnarled olive trees. They reminded me of little old men, bent and twisted. When seen against a ferocious storm, they became even more mysterious and mystical. This painting pleases me as much as the other displeased me."

Vincent

The auctioneer continued, "A diary will be auctioned along with the painting. This diary is by the hand of Juliette Martine, a favorite model, companion, and friend of Vincent van Gogh. The diary documents Van Gogh's gift of the painting to Martine. I will now read from Juliette's actual diary." He was handed white cotton gloves and put them on before taking the book from a gloved assistant.

July 23, 1889

To my surprise, a package arrived from Vincent today. I never get packages. I felt like I did as a small child on Noël, when I woke in the morning hoping there would be a small gift for me. I slowly unwrapped the cord and brown paper and found a painting and a note, which I laid aside. The sky in the painting is blue and black, but the dark clouds are all the same. The olive trees in the grove don't look normal and are funny colors. As he always does, Vincent has painted the name on the back. It says "Stormy Day in the Olive Grove" and his name, Vincent van Gogh. After a while, I open his note. He writes that the painting is a gift

237

to me and is a sister piece to the "Starry Night" painting he showed me when I visited him. He says it is a very stormy sky in an olive grove that might remind me of the one I knew as a child.

I touch the painting tenderly, as I would touch Vincent's skin. Oh, how I want to love this gift, but the colors seem so wrong. The whole painting is scary, and I hate it, but I can't tell him that. It makes me feel Vincent's pain.

Mon Dieu! My breath leaves me. Is that what Vincent is trying to say to me with this painting? I run my fingers across the dark sky. Is he trying to show me, to have me feel his pain, his sorrow? All this time, and I never knew. Can I ask him this? I will hang it here in my small room and think on this. Yes, I must think on this.

His note also says that "Stormy Day" is a gift for all my companionship and modeling, for which he could not pay. He signs it, "Fondly, your Vincent."

I think that I will treasure this note as much as the painting ... forever.

July 29, 1889

My Vincent died today. They told me his last moments were in his brother Theo's arms. I think he would have liked that. I know now that this strange man meant everything to me. I hurt for the loss of him. But now when I fall asleep at night, under my quilt, I will know he suffers no more. There is no more pain for my Vincent. My tears are leaving wrinkly spots on the pages in my book. The ink is running from my words, melting into the paper as my heart now melts into my soul.

I wonder if anyone will ever see or understand his art. He seemed to know what he wanted to say in his paintings but was unable to get others to see it through his eyes.

I want to believe that in the end, in "Stormy Day," I finally saw it. Maybe in that moment, Vincent, I finally saw you.

He paused for a minute or so to let these words sink in. "Now we begin the auction," he said, handing the book and then his gloves back to the waiting assistant. "Who will offer £80 million?"

Many paddles went up. The bidding was rapid and only slowed down when the price hit £110 million, but it didn't stop there. Ultimately the hammer fell on a price of £250 million, or about €280 million, plus of course, the buyer's premium. The buyer asked to remain anonymous.

When the hammer went down, the auctioneer said, "Congratulations! The bid went to a buyer on the phone. Ladies and gentlemen, it is my pleasure to announce that this is the highest auction price ever for a Van Gogh." The room erupted with applause.

The Martines were elated with the results. Now they had more than enough money to help themselves and their neighbors and friends, which they had pledged to do. They planned to continue harvesting olives on the family farm and do some traveling.

The anonymous buyer donated the artwork and the diary to the Louvre, with the stipulation that the diary must always be displayed with the work and that any and all acknowledgments must state: "Anonymous Gift Given in Honor of the Family of Juliette Martine."

ACKNOWLEDGMENTS

Many thanks to two special readers, Peter Blowers and Joan Dwyer, for their perceptive review and comments and thanks to Christopher Blowers who stimulated the descriptive color in Juliette's diary. A debt of gratitude is owed to Kathleen Kinkopf for the book cover art and design, Enrico Embroli for our portrait art and Ed Fong for the logo design. Special thanks to Josette Haddad for her copyediting and Melissa Bowersock for her help with Amazon publishing.

Thanks also to our gracious hosts: Linzi Kennaway Nolan in Kenya, where the first draft of this book was written, and Kathleen McPhail in Victoria, B.C., where the final draft was completed.

JULIETTE'S VAN GOGH

FACTS AND FICTION

FACT:

> Cities and landmarks are as described. Hotels and restaurants are fictitious, though modeled after actual facilities, and the menus are typical of the areas. Descriptions of the Pompidou and the Van Gogh Museum are somewhat embellished, while attempting to maintain the character of the facilities and their environs.

FACT:

> Vincent van Gogh was a masterful artist. He only sold one or two paintings during his lifetime, and for a pittance. His paintings now sell for many hundreds of millions of dollars. He did indeed cut off part of his ear in a fit of depression. He admitted himself into the asylum at Saint-Rémy, in France, and left of his own accord. He is reported to have committed suicide by shooting himself. Two excellent movies about Vincent van Gogh are Vincent van Gogh: Painted with Words (2010) and Loving Vincent (2017).

FACT:

> Vincent van Gogh wrote many letters to his brother Theo. In those letters, he does mention Starry Night. See The Complete Letters of Vincent van Gogh (3 volumes, Bulfinch Press,

2000) and The Letters of Vincent van Gogh (Penguin Classics, 1998).

FICTION:

There is no letter describing a painting called Stormy Day in the Olive Grove. The painting is pure fiction.

FACT:

Vincent van Gogh did have a favorite mistress and model. Her name was Clasina Maria Hoornik, or Sien.

FICTION:

The described model and companion, Juliette Martine, is purely fictional, as is her diary.

FACT:

The Van Gogh Museum in Amsterdam exists and is the authenticating body for Van Gogh's work. It does have a specific process for authenticating a work as being by Vincent van Gogh, which may include an actual presentation of the work at the museum.

FICTION:

Though the depiction of the Van Gogh Museum's authentication process is accurate to the best of my ability, the authentication board as presented in this novel is an imaginary group, as are the names of its members and employees.

FACT:

The Metropolitan Museum of Art in New York does indeed have a wonderful conservation department. If they employ a specialist in analyzing paint from old masters is not known by me.

FACT:

Insurance companies do exist that will insure and arrange secure transport for fine art. In the case of stolen or missing art, they may hire outside consultants who receive a portion of the art's value if recovered.

FICTION:

Pfyffer and Sons Insurance is a fictional insurance company. Whether insurance policies contain a provision that allows for transfer of ownership after the insurance company has paid a claim is unknown to me.

FACT:

The FBI has a division that deals with art-related crimes. The UN has been involved with the restitution of Nazi-looted art.

FICTION:

> SALT is a fictional company, as are its members.

FACT:

> There are countries where one can still obtain a numbered bank account. However, most (but not all) have signed agreements to turn over such information on request of various countries provided there is probable cause for the accounts to be associated with a crime. A few countries do not consider tax evasion such a crime.

FACT:

> The dark web exists, but I have no idea how to access it.

FACT:

> Leviticus 19:28, New International Version of the Old Testament reads, "Do not cut your bodies for the dead or put tattoos on yourselves."

FACT:

> The Centre Pompidou and L'Atelier des Lumières are real and as described. The exhibitions change. If you visit, check out their web-sites first.

FACT:

246

Touch DNA is a real thing, and advances in DNA sequencing leave many options open for future authentication possibilities.

FICTION:

To my knowledge, none of Van Gogh's art or artifacts have been tested for touch DNA, and therefore there is no database for comparison to undiscovered art; this is not to say that such a database could not be in progress.

JULIETTE'S VAN GOGH

Dear Reader:

Thank you for reading this novel. If you enjoyed it, we'd so appreciate your review on Amazon or your favorite book web-site. However brief, it would be valuable. Word of mouth is also very important to any author, any mention to your friends and social media contacts would go a long way towards the book's success.

You also might enjoy my first SALT novel, The Templars' Chalice available on Amazon in paperback and Kindle.

For more information about both books and both authors please visit my website, CLDecker.com, and sign up for our monthly newsletter. The blog on the web site will help you keep in touch with us and be among the first to learn of SALT's future adventures.

C.L.Decker/C.A.Scribner

JULIETTE'S VAN GOGH

Made in the USA
San Bernardino, CA
06 May 2020